FIGHTING PRIDE

deadly sins series

BY JENNIFER MILLER

ISBN: 978-0-9894074-6-5

Copyright © 2017

Cover designer - Robin Harper with Wicked by Design
Formatting - Elaine York, Allusion Graphics, LLC/
Publishing & Book Formatting, www.allusiongraphics.com
Editing - CDK & Associates
Cover - Adobe Stock

DEDICATION

To Tami - you are always on my mind and in my heart.
#fuckcancer

Life is tough my darling, but so are you. - *Stephanie Bennett-Henry*

"Sometimes you have to swallow your pride and accept that you're wrong. It's not giving up, it's growing up."
– *Author Unknown*

"Pride is a spiritual cancer: it eats up the very possibility of love, or contentment, or even common sense."
– *C.S. Lewis*

PROLOGUE

Cole

"Cole, something's wrong with the baby."

My mind is fuzzy as my sleep-filled eyes try to open in response to whatever has woken me. My surroundings slowly come into focus as I look around the room in confusion.

"Cole. Please wake up. Please. Something is wrong."

The fear in her voice immediately shakes the cobwebs from my mind and I bolt upright looking toward Tatum's spot on the bed and feeling alarm when I find it empty.

"Cole," she says my name again and I'm startled to find her standing next to my side of the bed. She's bent over at the waist holding her stomach. Pain is clearly evidenced on her face, but it's the terror in her eyes that has me instantly jetting out of bed. Wordlessly I help her sit on the side of the bed, then throw on the jeans and the shirt I had thrown over a chair only a few hours before.

"Wait here," I instruct her quickly as I run out of our bedroom toward the kitchen. Grabbing my car keys out of a bowl we keep on the counter, I grab the overnight bag Tatum packed weeks ago in preparation for the birth of our baby, and run it out to the car before I return for her. Scooping her in my arms I try to ignore the stabbing fear in my heart when she moans in pain from the movement. Carefully, I carry her from the apartment, somehow managing to close the door behind us, and into the parking lot as quickly as possible.

Locating my car in one of our two assigned parking spaces, I get the door open and place her gently inside. Reaching across her for the seatbelt, I pull it across her body and click it into place. Her eyes laced with fear meet mine. I give her what I hope is a reassuring smile, place a kiss on her forehead and run to my side of the car all the while apprehension makes the hairs on my neck stand at attention. Frustratingly, I drop the keys onto the floor mat, and scramble to find them and get them into the ignition. Sighing with relief as my temperamental car starts without a hitch, I drive with one hand and hold hers with the other. The entire way to the hospital emergency room I silently plead with god, repeatedly reciting prayers to please let the woman I love and the baby that already has our hearts be okay. I tell him I'll do anything, anything at all, if they will both just be okay.

This pregnancy isn't something we planned by any means. We sacrificed plans, modified our lives, made significant changes, and have become optimal impending parent students these past months to get ready for her arrival. We know it's a girl. We have the ultrasound pictures proudly displayed on our refrigerator that prove it.

The preparation was difficult, even exhausting at times, but necessary. Tatum decided not to go to art school and turned down the scholarship she had been offered and I dropped out of college and quit MMA fighting. There's no money to be made with fighting – at least not yet for me – I'm too new. I don't have the time to commit, given my new responsibilities. The path to success can be long and all encompassing and I haven't the luxury of such time right now. We need a steady income for our new family now. No, fighting wasn't in my cards, even if I thought otherwise. In an instant, Tatum and our child trumped everything. This pregnancy may not have been planned, but it was a blessing never the less. Tatum and our baby immediately became my number one priority. After all, they are the most important people in my life. I'd do anything or give up anything for both of them without question.

In the midst of my praying and reflection, I glance at Tatum and see her lips moving silently and I know she's doing the same thing. I'd like to offer her words of comfort, I want to tell her that everything will be okay, but one look at her obvious distress reinforces the struggle with finding the optimism needed to match the words. She knows me too well. She'd see right through any act I would try to perform. I fear it would only sound hollow if I tried. It's as if the words are held hostage in my throat, fear a barrier that's too strong for me to push the words through. Instead, I continue silently pleading with god instead.

Finally arriving at the hospital, relieved to have hit all green lights, I whip into the first parking space at the emergency entrance I find. Running to Tatum's side of the car, I lift her into my arms once again and rush through the waiting area to a reception desk taking care to not jostle her too much. "Help! Please, someone help us."

"Sir?" A nurse runs out from behind the counter and approaches me immediately, "What's the problem?" Her eyes move rapidly from me to Tatum and I can see her trying to assess the situation.

"My girlfriend. She's pregnant, but she's bleeding. A lot. Please help us."

Immediately the nurse springs into action, "Follow me!" I do so immediately, following her down the hallway. She opens a sliding glass door, moves a curtain aside, and gestures to the empty gurney. Placing Tatum down gently, she immediately reaches for my hand and squeezes, then holds it tightly in her own, tears running in silent rivers down her cheeks.

The nurse fires questions at her, "When did the bleeding start?"

"I'm not sure. I woke up because I felt cramping and went to the restroom. I found that I was bleeding and the cramping has only increased in intensity."

"How far along are you?"

"Thirty weeks."

"Rate your pain between one and ten, ten being severe."

"I don't know. An eight?" She struggles to breathe as she obviously breathes through pain.

It dawns on me that we have been walking through the corridors. We come to a set of doors and the nurse pushes an automatic opener on the wall. Entering what I realize is the labor area we toured once, other people in hospital scrubs surround us and direct us into a waiting room. We ease Tatum from the gurney onto a bed while a nurse begins to hook her up to various gadgets.

I move out of the way reluctantly letting go of Tatum's hand.

My eyes volley between the nurses and what they're doing, and Tatum's worried face. Each time she grimaces in pain, I can feel myself cringe in response. I'd give anything to take it from her. I've never felt more helpless.

A doctor joins and asks Tatum many of the same questions the nurses just asked. I find myself wanting to cry out in frustration, but refrain. "Sir, would you give us a few moments? We need to get this gown on her and complete our examination. We'll call you right back in as soon as we're finished."

I nod, walk to Tatum and kiss her forehead before leaving the room and begin pacing the hall outside her room. I try to remain calm; I try to think positive thoughts. I try to recall everything I've read since I found out she was pregnant. I've been fully enmeshed in this experience with her in any and every way possible. I researched and administered remedies and even sat with her and rubbed her back when she had horrible morning sickness. I've attended every doctor appointment. Made sure she took her vitamins. We took daily walks so she'd get exercise, but not too much and never anything strenuous. We've read books and internet articles. Hell, I've even shopped for baby items. Strange maybe, but important to me. I wrack my brain for anything that I may have read about this and come up empty. When they emerge and tell me I can go back inside, I breathe a sigh of relief to be at her side once more.

They've moved a large ultrasound machine to Tatum's bedside. They already have her gown up over her belly and the doctor is squeezing petroleum jelly onto her stomach.

There have been moments in my life that I know I will never forget. Hearing my mom cry over my absentee father. Meeting Jax and the guys. Getting accepted to college. The night I went to a dorm room to pick up my date only finding I was much more interested in her roommate instead, Tatum. Asking Tatum out over and over until she finally said yes. Our first kiss, and the first time we had sex. Winning my first MMA fight. Tatum telling me she's pregnant. Getting the call for my "real" job to support my new family. Hearing my baby's heartbeat for the first time and seeing the smile that lit up Tatum's face. And then, watching as the doctor moves the Doppler over Tatum's belly again and again and again, only to be met with silence, and Tatum's wail of pain.

CHAPTER ONE

Cole

"You're hitting like a goddamn girl," Jerry yells slurring his words.

There isn't a day that goes by where murdering him doesn't run through my mind. Does that concern me? Maybe a little. Would I ever do it? Hell to the fucking no. But does that mean I don't find the thoughts highly satisfying? Maybe I shouldn't answer that. Besides, I figure I'm entitled to use anything that can help me get through a day having to deal with him. So, I'll just keep enjoying thoughts of pounding his face into the ground.

Sweat pours down my body in waves but I barely pay it, or Jerry for that matter, any attention as I keep pounding the bag in front of me. I've been training for hours. I have a big fight coming up, one that could mean a big payday. A payday I'm desperate to receive. It's one step closer to getting out from under his thumb – my contracted obligation almost up – it's so close I can practically taste it. It's the much-needed light at the end of the tunnel. Especially since the metaphorical tunnel is full of jagged glass and muck I've been crawling and scraping my way through on a daily basis for five long years. I decided long ago the best thing to help me deal with it all would be to keep looking toward the end prize, and to save every fucking dollar I can. The end goal has become the reason I keep pounding, slamming and abusing my body into complete exhaustion day after day.

My arms burn, my fists sting under the tape they're wrapped in, and my muscles ache - begging for rest. I ignore them, relishing in the pain. When you live your life feeling like you're dead inside, this kind of pain helps remind me that I really am alive after all – at least physically. I push on, my goals giving me motivation to overpower the nasty voice in my ear that could care less about my exhaustion or state of mind. And doesn't have a clue what motivates me to push on.

"Punch it harder than that!" Jerry's demand whips at my ears like a lash. "You're such a goddamn pussy. Why do I even waste my time with you?" Internally, I laugh. We both know why. I'm his ticket inside the MMA since his son Jackson Stone has nothing to do with him.

With a roll of my eyes I ignore him, and quickly determine that a quick jab to his throat would do it. Sure, it wouldn't kill him, but it would be highly satisfying. I picture him coughing and hacking from the hit, grabbing at his throat, face redder than fire, eyes bulging, his voice, at least momentarily silent. That would be the best fucking part – I wouldn't have to hear his annoying yacking anymore – at least until he healed. Yesterday, I was convinced grabbing his balls and yanking until they burst out of their tiny sac or literally tore off in my hand and he bled out was the way to take him out. Before that, I just thought maybe a lit match held close to his body -maybe up to his fat ass - would do the trick. He's so fucking hairy; he'd quickly go up in flames. Yeah, I've definitely got issues. Oh well, most of us do, and we all find ways to help us deal. My lips curl at the corner of my mouth at my thoughts. No way in hell I'd ever do any of it, but sometimes imagining it helps me get through the worst moments.

"Are you fucking listening to me? I said punch the bag harder. What do you think this is, fucking patty cake? You wimp! How do you expect to win if you don't even have the stamina to punch a bag for a few hours?" Jerry yells then sighs loudly, shaking his head in exasperation.

He knows damn well how long I've been here. Sometimes I think he just bitches to bitch. It doesn't help that he's been drinking.

The slurring of his words and his unstable stature make it clear he's had more than a few. I should have just hit up Jax's gym today, god knows I'd much rather be working out with my friends. Jax, a friend since high school, as well as Tyson, Ryder, Dylan, Zane, and Levi all work out at Jax's gym, XTreme Fitness Center. Jerry used to coach me there, but after a nasty run in with his son Jax, Jerry was kicked out of the gym so I spend more time here than I'd like.

He continues to spit useless words my way and I block them out the best I can and power on. I try to ignore the fucked up methods he uses to train me. Part of it is that I'm his ticket to piss off the son that he's dying to take revenge against. He wants to try and build me up to become even stronger and better than Jax. He's delusional. But, unfortunately, I have no choice but to simply endure in this existence. It's one I created for myself, the reason far bigger and far more important than enduring the asshole in my ear.

Using my forearm to swipe the sweat dripping from my forehead, I back away and drop my arms. "What the fuck are you doing, boy? Did I say you were done?" Turning to Jerry, I give him a look. One that says I'm done and don't fuck with me. The one that even he knows when to back down from. He clears his throat, "Fine. Get your ass back here tomorrow bright and early."

I almost laugh. Given the liquor he's clearly putting down, he won't be here early and he knows it. Instead, I choose not to waste words on him and stalk off to the locker room for a much needed shower. Turning the water on, I strip while waiting for it to warm. Looking down at myself I take in the artwork decorating my body. The story of my life can be found in my tattoos. Happiness, sadness, hopes, accomplishments, all of it right here like a priceless canvas. I showcase the things that have made me who I am, good or bad. I run my hand over the taped wrapped hands on my side, the heart pierced with a writing pen on the inside of my bicep, a cross on the back of my shoulder, and a rose for my mom on my arm. Brushing my hand over the name I wear across my ribs, my finger traces each letter in her name, turning my thoughts somber.

With burning eyes, I quickly wash and dress, hurriedly packing my bag, anxious to get the hell out of the gym. Standing on the sidewalk for a few minutes I breathe in the smell of rain in the air. It doesn't rain much in Arizona, but when it does, it's like a party. Everyone gets excited and revels initially at the smell of the impending downpour and then the feeling of it on skin.

I start my car and immediately crank up the radio hoping to drown out my somber thoughts. I mindlessly drive and arrive at my apartment door ready to insert the key into the lock, but pause when I hear laughter. Looking down toward my friend Ryder's apartment I smile a little unable to help but feel happy for him. I like living in the same building, and it used to be pure entertainment seeing the women come and go from his apartment. He definitely had a revolving door, that's for sure, but not anymore. He and his girl Tessa are really happy together and I see him smile more that I ever have. Well, when I see him anyway. Tessa moved in with him recently, and while I miss hanging out with my friend on what was sometimes a nightly basis, it's a good thing and I'm happy for both of them.

I could be wrong, but I suspect that he stayed in his apartment here instead of moving into Tessa's nicer one for a reason – me. I mean, sure, Jax's gym isn't far from here and Ryder works out daily so it makes sense he would want to stay close by, but I think my friend is worried about me. I wish he wouldn't be. Nothing he can do about it. And he has much better things to focus on anyway.

Unlocking my door, I set my stuff down and look around. The dark space feels especially uninviting tonight, almost sterile. Earlier, all I wanted to do was come home, crack open a beer and catch the end of the ball game, but now, I don't feel much like being here at all. Before I give it another thought, I spin on my heel, lock the door once more and head out – Ryder and Tessa's laughter following me down the hall.

Forgoing driving, I elect to walk instead. Turning right, I head toward the busy part of down town. Taking a deep breath my body slowly relaxes – my shoulders ease, fists unclench, even my jaw loosens.

My apartment building is located on Mill, which is near the local college. With school in session right now, the street is busy. Restaurants have people spilling out the doors, stores stay open later and shoppers move in and out. Laughter floats on the air and I can hear music from a local band playing in the plaza that's the center of it all. The threat of rain isn't keeping people inside tonight.

It's impossible not to enjoy the electricity in the air. Tucking my hands in my pockets, I continue my walk, eyeing an ice cream store contemplating if I want to take in the calories or not. Before I can make up my mind, a young kid on my right smiles and hands me a flyer, "Here you go, sir."

Reaching out, I automatically take it from him, nodding in return. I take several steps deciding I'd like that ice cream after all before I look down absently at the flyer in my hand intending to dump it in the trash can on my way inside the parlor. I'm expecting it to be for a sale at one of the local stores on this street, or maybe an advertisement for a performance of some kind, but what I see instead makes me feel like I've been stabbed in the chest with an ice pick. My breath stalls in my chest and I come to a complete stop, unable to move.

My eyes blink over and over and my hand begins to shake as I stare down at the paper trying to comprehend what I'm seeing. There's writing, but it's the eyes staring at me from the photo in the bottom right corner that sears my very soul. Beautiful, even in black and white, I take in the slight curve of her full lips as she smiles at whoever is behind the lens. In my mind, I see the blue and green of her eyes as if she's dazzling me with them right now. Reaching out a finger, I trace the line of her jaw, my hand forming a fist after I reach her chin.

Looking away, I take a moment to gather myself and simply breathe. It takes a moment for me to realize the foreign feeling occurring is my heart beating out of control in my chest. It's been far too long since I've felt it, I've forgotten I even have one. It seems that it shriveled up and died five years ago.

Seeing a bench to my left, I quickly take a seat and close my eyes, trying to center myself, refusing to acknowledge the burning behind my eyes. Squeezing my eyes tight once more, I open them and dare to look again at the flyer making sure this isn't some crazy dream. I look at her face again, but briefly this time, then move my eyes to read the text. It's an announcement for an art show. It's for her work – her paintings. Pride, that I have no right to feel, bursts through my chest. She did it. I knew she would. I knew she could.

And the show, it's here in downtown Tempe at a gallery literally on the same street where I'm sitting. Looking down the street in the direction of the gallery, I startle when I see the lit sign from my seat. It shines like a beacon from the overhang in front of the front door, enticing, inviting. I stare at it, for I'm not sure how long. I wrestle with the decision in my mind. My chest begins to ache at the thought of seeing her again. Memories begin to flood my mind, but I push them away, not able to handle them. Not able to think about her. To think about the last time I saw her. When I broke her.

Before I even realize what I'm doing I'm moving rapidly down the sidewalk. Some part of my mind calls out to me, trying initially to stop me, then to slow my steps, another part second-guesses each footstep, but I ignore it all and continue to put one foot in front of the other. Walking has never been so difficult. Stopping suddenly, the reality of what I'm doing hits and I turn and quicken the pace back toward my apartment. What the hell am I thinking? What if she sees me? What would I even say? Do I even have a right to see her? Would she even acknowledge seeing me? My heart races at the thought and I press my hand there. Do I want her to see me? Do I want to talk to her? I have so much shit I'd like to say to her, but even more I'd like to hear in return. Is she happy? Has she thought about me at all these past five years? Does she still hate me? She should. I still hate me.

Somehow, I've made my way back toward the gallery and find myself standing feet from the front. Taking a deep breath, I fold the flyer up into several squares and shove it in my pocket, then clear my throat. There's a large window, giving art lovers a peek at the gallery exhibits from the sidewalk in hopes of invoking enough interest to entice entry. I notice the lights are on and the glow brightens the sidewalk before it. Moving to the edge of the window, I peek in, keeping most of my body to the side.

My eyes move rapidly around the room, looking for her. There are people working, moving around the room, large canvases in their arms. It looks as if they are setting up for the showing that according to the flyer begins tomorrow. I want to see her work too, but I can't focus on it right now, all I can do is look for her.

A movement in the far right corner of the room captures my attention. A woman in black has her back to me, she's facing a painting that I can't see, but I'd recognize that body, her stance, that hair - anywhere. My breath catches, my fists clench, my teeth grind together and pain mixed with shock and longing runs through my body making me clench my muscles as if doing so helps fight off the sizzling pain that engulfs me. My hand grips the edge of the window, the stucco of the building ripping skin, and I find myself practically pressed against the glass, as if I'm trying to get even closer to her. Tears unashamedly flood my eyes without my permission and I blink rapidly against them in automatic reflex. I open my mouth, but for what? To say her name? To scream 'I'm sorry' over and over again?

Her head turns suddenly as if something has captured her attention, but I can't take my eyes off of her to see what it is. It isn't until an arm goes across her shoulders that he captures my attention. When she smiles at him, the sight of it burns its way through my body. When she lifts her head up to his and he places a kiss on her lips, bile floods my throat and just as I swear she turns her head toward me, I turn and run back to my apartment, hoping to leave the pain in my veins far behind.

CHAPTER TWO

Tatum

It feels strange to be back in this town. Now that I'm here, the past can no longer be kept in the recesses of my mind. It seems like only yesterday when I packed up my bags with tears in my eyes and anger and devastation in the depths of my very soul. I didn't want to leave here initially. Not because I didn't have a desire to start over, but because it felt like I was leaving my heart behind. I may have felt desperation for a change, and a longing to forget, but it was my heart full of Hope that somehow helped me push forward and leave when I did. Being away from here made the distance easier – better in some ways. I used to say that it would take Jesus himself to ever bring me back. But yet, here I am.

I knew being back would feel...strange. I was delusional when I assumed that the chapters of my life spent here with all of their emotions would remain in the past. That it wouldn't touch me or burden me all these years later. I couldn't have been more wrong. Even though it's been five years, I've experienced a searing pain resonating to the depth of my very bones since the moment my plane landed in this desert.

"This piece is hauntingly beautiful, ma'am."

Snapped out of my musings, I look at one of the gallery workers standing before one of my paintings. It's a woman looking in the mirror. Her hands are pressed against her flat stomach and tears pour down her face. You can almost see the harrowing pain and sorrow in her eyes, but outside the window where she stands is a lush garden. It's full of flowers, greenery, birds and *life*. A nest of baby birds is in a tree and the mother leans down to feed them. It's part of my 'Beautifully Broken' collection. It depicts how life moves on even when one feels otherwise; how there is always beauty in the midst of pain.

"Thank you," I murmur to the woman, shy about my own work and humbled by compliments after all this time.

Returning my focus to the group of paintings in front of me, my eyes move from piece to piece. I absorb the vivid and loving brush strokes. I wonder if admirers will be able to see my tears mixed into the paint. If they can see and feel the emotion poured into each and every one. The more I gaze at them, the stronger my inclination to take them down, conceal them. I want to hide them, take them totally out of view, as if in doing so, I can pretend this all never happened. This level of vulnerability leaves me feeling excruciatingly raw. It's as if I'm holding my life, my heart in my hands and laying it bare for everyone to look at, touch, judge and feel. Perhaps I'm not ready for this. As my chest tightens, agonizing with emotion, I realize I may never really be ready.

"You're second-guessing yourself again." Turning my head toward his voice, I smile at the man in my life. I find it a complete conundrum that at the same time Blaine can know me so well, in many ways, he doesn't know me at all. He places an arm around my shoulders and regardless of my thoughts I'm happy for the contact. Especially when I feel like I'm floundering. "They are beautiful," he reassures me, "and part of the process of moving forward."

Not wanting to dissect his words, I push them aside and lift my head to him in silent request for a kiss. He graces my lips with his for a moment, then pulls away with a smile.

Feeling as if I'm being watched, movement out of the corner of my eye grabs my attention. Turning my head to the window at the front of the gallery, there appears to be someone peering inside, but it's dark outside and very bright in here in contrast; I have trouble making out their characteristics. When the shadow moves, something in my heart stills for a moment and I think...but it can't be. Exhaling as the person walks away, I'm curious as to why I feel so unsettled. It's a busy street and people have been walking by all evening as we've been setting up. Pushing my feelings away, I tell myself I'm being silly and turn back to my painting collection.

My feelings see-saw between wanting to keep these pieces private and all to myself, to knowing that exposing them is truly a part of moving forward. For me, and for her. Besides, it's irrelevant at this point, the night before the showing. I long since committed to this, and many other showings for that matter. I just don't know what I was thinking agreeing to have a show here, of all places.

Yes you do. You are hoping to see him.

Slamming the door shut on that thought, I force concentration on Blaine's words instead. The rational side of me understands where he's coming from. Blaine would know best of course since after all, he's my therapist. Well, he *used* to be my therapist, before we became lovers. I know he's trying to help and be supportive, but sometimes I want to tell him he doesn't have a fucking clue. That not everything is purely clinical. That he should stop using his textbook psychobabble shit on me. I want to remind him that I'm not his patient anymore. The worst is when he speaks to me in his 'I'm trying to help you' voice. Sometimes I want to see what he would say if I told him that maybe I don't want to move forward. Maybe I like, or at least liked, much of my past. Maybe I don't want to do this and I think it's the worst idea ever. What would he think of that?

Actually, it wouldn't matter at all. He'd just tell me that what I'm feeling is normal, but not appropriate at this step in the therapeutic process, and blah blah. Sometimes I just want him to yell and fight back; to show some humanity about the events of my past life. Instead he's this calm, patient and rational man that seems to never lose his cool. I used to always think that it was exactly what I needed. I was done with the passionate, fiery, insanity inducing kind of man. An even keel personality was what I needed. Right? Maybe I'm wrong.

Suddenly feeling shock and discomfort at my thoughts, I remind myself that this self-talk is contrary to what I've come to know. I'm wrong. He's exactly what I need. He's secure, comfortable and reliable. He's helped me to move from my emotions, to move from dreams to reality. And that's a good thing. I'm being a jerk, especially since I know he's only trying to help. Smiling at him when he returns from giving direction to an employee that had a question, I firmly squeeze his arm, finally responding to his previous comment. "I know it's part of moving forward, I remember. But even though I know it, it doesn't mean that it's an easy thing to do. In fact, it's not at all an easy thing to do."

"Letting go never is. But, it's necessary."

Is it? I wonder to myself. What if I don't want to let go? Who says I have to? Why do I have to? I've moved past the unhealthy part of dealing with my loss and devastation as much as I can. The thoughts of her aren't debilitating any longer, and my paintings have helped me heal in an amazing and special way, but why do I feel like his version of 'moving on' is different from mine? I don't want to move on if it means asking me to forget. Because, I *never* want to forget, and sometimes I'm afraid I will. I'm afraid that she will no longer be a part of me, that I'll forget the perfect way her eyes tilted up in the corners, how soft the wisps of hair on her tiny head were, or the fullness of her bottom lip. I'd rather she always be a part of me, the best part, a beautiful part, the part that reminds me I'm strong and brave. Maybe that's what he means, but he never says that, he always says I have to 'move on' and 'let go'.

Blain interrupts my thoughts; "I think they've got this under control. They have the lay out sheet that tells them where the last of the paintings need to be placed."

"That may be so, but they still have had questions."

"I'm sure it's because you're here. If you weren't, they'd just move along and get the job done. Besides, we need to get you back to the hotel so you can rest. Tomorrow night is a big night." I start to argue but he places his finger over my lips and I frown. "Once we come here tomorrow and see that everything is set up perfectly, I have to leave remember?"

"Yes. I still don't understand why you have to leave before I actually have my showing. I'd like you to be here."

He sighs and pulls away, "We've discussed this already. You know that I need to get back to see some patients. And your being here without me is part of the process – you need to do this without me. Stand on your own capable legs. My physical support would be an obstacle, a crutch at this point in your healing. You know we've discussed this and agreed. I'll make sure everything is perfect before I leave and head to the airport."

"Just because I know the reason you're leaving, doesn't mean I have to like it."

"Of course not," he smiles. "You are entitled to your feelings. In fact, I'd expect nothing less." I'm not sure if he means that as fondly as I'd like to think he does. "Now let's go. We'll be here early enough tomorrow that if anything needs to be rearranged we can get it taken care of."

"Okay," I reluctantly agree. Looking around the room, I ascertain that they do have most everything finished and that is the only reason I agree to head out. He leads me through the gallery by the hand, and we exit through the back door and head toward our rental car.

I breathe in deeply as soon as we step outside, and sigh happily at the smell of rain in the air. The last five years in Chicago, and the hustle and bustle of city life, have made me forget the things I loved about living here. Not to mention the prominent smells in Chicago, in the thick of the city depending on where one is and the time of day, are exhaust fumes and the stench of trash. Though, I guess in more pleasant areas there's the smell of popcorn, hot dogs or even chocolate. Clearly, not the same, and while some may love it just fine, to me, Arizona wins hands down. Other things I missed are how pleasant the evenings are this time of year here. How beautiful the bougainvillea and cactus are when they're in bloom. Even the artistic sides of the highways and vegetation lined midways. How quiet the desert is at night, and the beautifully clear sky that gives you a spectacular view of the millions of stars in the sky. My memories of Arizona sunrises and sunsets don't do the real thing justice. But somehow, it's the smell of rain that will always remind me of stolen kisses and whispered promises.

As Blaine drives us back to our hotel, my eyes take in every detail as we drive, wanting to commit it all to memory so I never forget it again. Feeling like I need to apologize to my home for allowing myself to do so in the first place. I think I realize for the first time that no matter where I go, my heart will always find Arizona to be its home.

When Blaine first surprised me with the gallery showing I was angry. He told me he was friends with the owner of several galleries along the west coast, one of them in Arizona. He went behind my back and sent copies of my work to his friend Mark, and Mark sent an email to Blaine with an offer for me to do a gallery tour. I, along with my work of course, would appear at all of the galleries over the span of a couple weeks, having public showings at each. Some of my paintings would travel with me from gallery to gallery as a display of my work. Other pieces would be offered for sale. Many would be shipped in advance to the various galleries awaiting the show. He practically agreed before I knew a thing about it.

So, of course I was initially angry at him. But, I realize now that it was done out of love for me. It's both exciting and terrifying. I've had several showings in Chicago before, it was a mandatory part of my schooling, but nothing of this caliber, and it feels altogether different having a showing here. When Mark contacted me with the offer that he had already discussed with Blaine, I was on board for every stop but this one. But, a longing to visit my home, and the fact that it coincided with an important date in my life, seemed like it was fate telling me to visit. Five years away was long enough – a visit way overdue.

Blaine takes an unexpected turn down a street and I find that suddenly I'm staring at the old apartment complex where I used to live. The apartment bedroom faced the entrance to the complex and I can pinpoint exactly which apartment was mine, my eyes riveted to the window as if I can see my past self sitting there looking out the window. As we move past, balloons waving in the breeze that are tied to the entrance welcoming potential residents catch my attention and illicit a memory of the last time I watched balloons floating from that same sign fly in the air.

I'm not sure how long I've been trying to read, but I keep staring at the same spot, not really taking any of it in. It doesn't seem to be helping me today. I'm not sure why. Reading usually helps take the pain away. Burying my thoughts and feelings into another world helps. Losing myself in the pain of fictional characters makes me forget my own, at least for a little while. I've learned that keeping my mind busy is helpful – schoolwork is also really good for that. But sometimes it doesn't matter what I do.

Thoughts of her, of losing her, of missing her, of aching for her so much my arms literally move to hold her but find themselves wrapped around myself instead, overwhelm me. Each day feels like I lose her all over again. She'd be three months now. The baby books say that her milestones this month would be improving neck and upper body strength. She would have enough lower body strength to kick what I know would be her chubby little legs. Her hands would be opening and closing and she would be reaching for and grabbing at toys. I imagine her little hand closing around my fingers. How her skin would feel against mine as I nurse her, how she would fit perfectly in my arms, how I would revel in every sigh, laugh, smile, gurgle, and cry. I know that each and every day would have been better because somehow I managed to help create something so perfect; so divine. Except it's not, because she's not here. And I ache so deep and so vast that I don't even remember what it feels like to not feel this pain. At least with the pain I know that it was real, that she was real. I know that she wasn't just something I imagined. A beautiful dream.

Cole doesn't know it, but I kept a bunch of her things. We gave a lot of it away – well Cole did. He boxed it up and took it out of here. He didn't say so, but I think it bothered him when I would sit in her room among her things and cry. We didn't have much, but what we had was precious – like the soft, pink blanket I cling to now. I'm not sure if he did me a favor or if it only made things worse. I had placed a few items in my room, so when the other things disappeared, they remained. Otherwise, I'd be left with nothing other than the pieces of paper they gave me at the hospital that had imprints of her tiny hands and feet on them. I've traced those little lines with my finger tip over and over and over again.

I attend the counseling sessions arranged by the hospital and Cole. After class I rush there only to sit quietly and listen to Dr. Weisman tell me that what I'm feeling is normal and that this will pass, that her loss – this grief- will get easier. It takes all I have not to put my hands over my ears and scream at Dr. Weisman to shut up. What the hell would he know about losing a child he carried and so desperately wanted anyway? Does he understand that I either want to sleep forever, or am unable to sleep at all? Does he know how hard it is to go to class and study and concentrate on anything but her? What does he really know about this profound yearning for my daughter, this intense emptiness? Does he know how it feels to have had your body fail; to completely be unable to do the one thing we were created to do? Does he know how it feels to wonder why I had to be the one given a body that doesn't even work right? He has no fucking idea, and Cole doesn't understand why I find the sessions unbearable.

The rational part of me knows he's concerned, I know that he wants me to get better and to find the will to heal and move past this, but I simply don't know how. At least recently I've somehow found the will power to get up, get dressed for class, attend them and turn in my assignments and paintings on time. And even though it has taken every bit of strength I have most days, I returned to work – a job at the library on campus. It's not a big deal, but it's still a job, still a responsibility that I'm managing to follow through on. Sometimes it feels like I'm just going through the motions, sure, but I show up. That has to count for something.

The door to the apartment opens and closes and I fumble with what to do with the blanket I'm holding, and it isn't long before Cole finds me in our room. I look up at him and even force a smile on my lips, "Hi. How was class?"

His eyes rake me head to toe and his brow furrows in a look of concern he seems to always wear anymore. The last few days his eyes have been full of sorrow, even more than they have the last few months and I have a feeling he wants to say something, but he doesn't.

"It was fine." His hand moves and I notice a white open envelope in his hand, his fingers white from grasping it so tightly.

"What's that?" I ask gesturing to the envelope.

"It's mail. For you."

"And you opened it?" I ask confused. He never opens my mail. He runs a hand through his hair and walks to one side of the room and then back again. He opens his mouth to say something and then closes it again. After this is repeated a few times I put my book down and lean forward, "Cole, spit it out. What's going on?"

"I want you to go."

"Go?" I ask confused.

"Yes. I think you should go. No, I know you should go."

"What are you talking about?"

He hands me the envelope and when I see the return address my heart stutters in my chest and my brows lower in confusion. It's from the

Institute of Art, an art school in Chicago, IL that I had applied for. But not just any art school, it was my first choice, before I elected to stay here and attend the art program at Arizona State University. I just couldn't afford my first choice. Slowly, I take the letter out of the envelope, almost afraid to open it and see what it says. Words and phrases stand out at me but it takes a moment for my mind to catch up. Phrases like, 'opening still available', 'transfer of credits', 'full ride scholarship' and 'in two weeks'. Looking at Cole, my confusion quickly fades away as the look on his face says it all. "You think I should go," I repeat his words.

He stares at me for a long time, his eyes not leaving mine. I wish I could define all the emotions I see run across his face, but the jumble of them confuse me. I know I see sadness and maybe fear but the one that stands out at me the most is severe determination. "I want you to go."

"But, it's in Chicago," I tell him lamely. He nods. "I'd have to leave. I mean, obviously I would. It's far away." Again, he nods. "Cole, I don't… I'm confused. I don't even know how or why I have a scholarship. This doesn't make any sense."

"Does it matter? This is an opportunity you can't pass up. I won't let you, Tatum. It's exactly what the doctor says you need – what he said you would find – a way to work through your grief. A goal, something to focus on."

"No. I'm not going to leave Cole. I can't. I can't leave you. Besides, I only have one year left here, and my goal is to finish this program. To graduate."

"That's a better offer and you know it. Not only will they hopefully transfer your credits from here, but they are offering you a full ride to attend their graduate program as well."

"That just… that doesn't make any sense. I didn't even apply…"

"Tatum," Cole says my name sharply stopping my confused thoughts, "the one thing that you have still been able to do since… since…" he swallows hard and I look away, unable to see the pain on his face. My eyes flood with tears, while guilt and shame sit in my belly like a flesh eating

disease, threatening to eat me alive. I blink over and over furiously trying to push the tears back. "It's the one thing that you are still passionate about."

"That's not-"

"Yes. It is. It's the only time I see happiness in your eyes anymore. You need to go. I want you to go."

"You want me to go?" I repeat lamely again. It seems to be the only thing I clearly understand, but I shake my head. "No, no Cole. I won't leave you. I love you and I won't go." When I see him begin to shake his head again, I feel panic begin to tighten my chest. "Please, please, Cole. I promise. I promise I will get better. Tomorrow, maybe tomorrow I can even go out to dinner. Would you like that? We can even catch a movie or something too. I'm trying. I swear I am. It will get better. I'm sorry. I've just been so sad."

"I need you to go." His voice comes out louder than before and I immediately quit talking. My eyes devour his face; I try to take in every single twitch and assign it meaning. "Tatum," his voice breaks on my name and it takes him a moment to continue. "I can't do this anymore."

A sob instantly chokes back other words and a noise escapes my throat and it feels as if my chest is going to cave in on itself in panic and despair. "What?" I ask. A mere whisper compared to the storm going on inside of me.

"I can't do this anymore. I can't...I can't look at you, like this, day after day. We are just feeding off of each other's guilt and pain and sorrow. Instead of bringing us together it's pushing us apart and I can't live like this anymore. I can't – I can't do this anymore."

"You can't do this anymore," I repeat lamely, the words feeling strange on my tongue.

"I need you to call them and tell them that you will move to Illinois, that you will take this full ride scholarship, and you will finally live out the dream you had before....before..."

Funny how he's quick to point out my failings yet he can't even utter the words himself. He continues to speak and make excuses and gives me *reasoning for his feelings, but I don't hear any of it, not really. This feels like one more loss, one more thing to overcome. A motion out the window catches my eye and I look out the window to see pink balloons flying in the sky yet bound by the string that holds them to the sign at the front of our apartment complex entrance. It's almost as if they are a sign from Hope, silly as that may seem. Like she's telling me to cut the string, to reach for the sky; to not let myself be bound any longer by this pain and heartache.*

It won't be easy, but I can do it. And I will. For her.

"We're here," Blaine says snapping me out of my thoughts. Looking around I realize we've parked and the car is no longer running. Glancing at him I wonder how many times he may have spoken to me before I became aware of it – trapped in thoughts from long ago. Smiling at him, I open my door and step out of the car. "You okay?" he asks as he comes around to my side and takes my hand.

"Fine."

He squeezes my hand and doesn't ask me any further questions and I'm relieved. Following him into the hotel, it occurs to me that even though being here is harder than I expected given the fact I've certainly moved on with my life, I feel comfort in knowing that I've accomplished exactly what I said I would do, for her, yes, but also for me. I just wish that I felt content instead of this unsettled feeling that I can't seem to shake.

Once inside our room, Blaine turns to me and gives me a look that I know the definition of before he even touches me. I force a smile I don't feel, and tell myself that I'll be okay. This life of mine is a good one, flaws and all. I'm just feeling on edge because I'm nervous about the showing tomorrow night. That's all this is. I'm sure of it. I'm happy.

Why does it feel like I'm trying too hard to convince myself?

CHAPTER THREE

Cole

I am not happy. I should not be back here and I don't know what the hell I'm doing. I've argued with myself about it all day long. I saw her through the window yesterday, she smiled, she looked… amazing, but most importantly she looked happy. That should be enough. Yet somehow, it isn't. I feel greedy for more. Seeing her brings back feelings I haven't had in years. Or have not been able to confront for years. Feelings of want, desire and need for her, but also traces of my old self deep inside. The person that went after what he wanted and took it, or at least worked like hll to get it.

I keep telling myself I only want one more look. Just one. I want to make sure that the smile I saw yesterday is genuine. I want to see for myself that her eyes are shining in the way I remember so well. The way that tells me she's happy, in love, and loving her life. The way she used to smile before we lost our baby. The smile I used to be afraid that I would forget, but found it impossible since it appeared in my dreams regularly.

Of course I'm not sure how I'll be able to know any of these things for sure because my plan involves her never even seeing me. Part of me would do anything to have her eyes look into my own again, but that's not possible. Anyway, I just want one more glimpse, one more look. How could I not? She's here. In Arizona. In our home once more. After five long years of wondering about her, I can see her for myself. And my god, she's right down the street, I couldn't resist my desire to see her even if I tried. I'm not strong enough. I've been strong for all these years, I more than deserve this.

I couldn't concentrate all day long. I'm pretty sure Jerry has never yelled at me more than he did today, and that's saying something. He even took a swing at me in what is becoming his daily drunken state telling me that it would help, "snap me out of whatever the hell is wrong with me." Little does he know that isn't possible. And I don't even want to think about what he would do if he knew that she was here, or if he knew what I was doing right now. God knows what he would threaten me with, and the thought makes my stomach clench. But still, the lure to see her is stronger.

As soon as it was appropriate, I made an excuse about not feeling well and got the hell out of the gym. I've been pacing my apartment all afternoon wishing the time would move faster. I even showered twice hoping the warm water would soothe my nerves. Part of it was also because I kept imagining myself walking in here and taking Tatum in my arms because I simply wanted one more hug, one more touch, one more moment, one more *anything* with her. But the fact is, I lost my right to have anything with her long ago. I signed those rights away literally, and while a piece of me regrets it, I would make the same decision again.

It's been fucking painful, all this time, missing her, aching for her, wondering about her and clinging to hope that it was the right thing. That she wouldn't just throw the opportunity away. But here she is…a gallery showing. She's made it. She really has. I knew she had the ability to from the very first moment I saw her painting. The memory comes to my mind immediately.

Making my way up the stairs of the co-ed dormitory, I walk to the door I'm seeking and knock loudly. I'm anxious to pick up Chelsea with the double d's and take her out. Ever since I met her in the course we share together I've been working my way to get my hand under that shirt of hers and on what promised to be one hell of a naked view. I'm taking her out to dinner and a movie tonight, but I'm hoping we can skip the movie and get comfy in the back seat of my car instead.

When the door swings open, a gorgeous brunette with stunning green, or maybe they're blue, eyes opens the door. She looks annoyed if the pinched look on her face is any indication. Her hair is piled on top of her head but a few pieces fall down her face the bottoms landing on the top of her exposed right shoulder. She has something dark smeared on her face in a few places, and her hand is on her hip. "What?" she snaps at me and all I can do is simply stare at how beautiful she is, but she's not about to let that happen. She slams the door in my face.

Knocking again, it opens quickly and she just stares at me as if I'm the stupidest person she's ever seen. "Hi, I'm Cole. I'm here for Chelsea," I finally manage to say.

"She's in the bathroom, probably putting on her eighteenth coat of mascara," she says then walks away from the door leaving it open.

Walking inside, I barely register much of the small dorm because I'm too interested in watching the spit fire that answered the door. She's moved to her side of the room and sits before the window. She has the curtains pulled open and in front of the window she has a large easel set up and she's standing before it. Clearly, she's painting which explains the smears of color on her face. As I walk around her, I don't think twice about invading her privacy and look at her canvas, then look at her.

"Stare much?" she asks sarcastically without turning to look at me.

"You're really good at that," I tell her gesturing to the painting and ignoring her sarcastic comment. And I mean it. She's captured the image of the sky perfectly. The brightness of the moon almost seems to shine with light from her canvas. She's captured the smokiness of the clouds around it and somehow the rest of the sky almost seems to glow. I have no idea how she's managed to make a painting look so full of light, but it's really beautiful, but it's nothing compared to her. I couldn't look away if I wanted to. So, I guess I am staring.

"Well, I should hope so since I work at it day and night and go to art school."

"Hell woman, who pissed in your cheerios? I gave you a compliment. Could you be more bitchy?"

"Do you want to find out?"

She stares at me and I can't get over how much of an attitude she has. I don't know what it is, but I find myself more amused than anything else. I can feel my lips curve into a smile, and I'm almost shocked when hers do too. We both start laughing out loud and honestly, I'm not even sure why, but I know that right there I vow to hear her laugh again.

"What's so funny?"

We both stop laughing when Chelsea opens the door and walks into the room. She looks great, but suddenly, her double d's aren't so appealing. Not as much as the little Monet that's captured my attention.

"Nothing," my new artist friend says to her roommate.

"I'm sure that's true," Chelsea says with a roll of her eyes. "Sorry you had to endure my boring roommate. I hope you weren't here long."

Ahh, the bane of college life. Getting stuck with a roommate that you don't get along with. Poor Monet, I think to myself.

"You two have a great time," she says with little sincerity. She turns back to her painting, but I can see her looking at me out of the corner of her eye.

"Actually, I don't think I'm feeling much like going out after all, Chelsea. I'm sorry."

"What? Are you serious?" She walks to me and places her hand on my head. I want to push her away, but I remain still. "You feel fine, no fever. Are you sure?"

"I'm sure that I am definitely wanting to take out the wrong roommate." Chelsea's mouth falls open and so does Monet's.

"Excuse me?" Chelsea asks, a look of indignity on her face.

"Did you need me to speak slower?" I ask her. I know it's mean, but she was a bitch to Monet and it pissed me off. Turning to my little painter, I smile and ask, "What's your name? Or should I just call you Monet, which is the name I've been calling you in my head."

She smiles and shakes her head in what I think is disbelief because she answers, "Tatum."

"Well Tatum, it's a pleasure to meet you. You will definitely be seeing me soon." I give her a quick wink and walk out of the room, but not before seeing her lips curve into a smile.

She's certainly earned the nickname Monet now, that's for sure.

Lingering outside I watch as the gallery gets more and more crowded by the minute. I'm in awe at the turn out, and happy this means Tatum will likely have a good night. I'm happy even more because I think that there are now enough people that I can hide within their presence.

Once inside, I exhale a deep breath. My chest feels tight and there are definitely nerves dancing in my stomach. Looking around the room, I try to find her. I want to make sure that when I see her, it's from a distance again. Not finding her among the crowd, I turn my attention to the paintings surrounding me and it isn't long before I get lost in them.

The paintings seem to be grouped in themes. There's various paintings of Chicago and I can tell the city has become one she loves. My favorites are the ones of Arizona. The desert in bloom is so defined it's as if I could live inside of it. There are paintings of streets after the rain, lush gardens, sunrises and sunsets. She has it all, something for everyone. There's a crowd around what must be the featured paintings for the show. Given the large display, their position in the gallery, and the lights surrounding them to show off the display, it's clear they must be the highlight of her work. Looking around for her again, and feeling frustrated that I still can't find her, I maneuver through people until I can finally see the display.

And I simply stop breathing.

My eyes can't take in every painting fast enough. Then I stop and start at the beginning again, devouring each image, taking in every detail. Tears burn behind my eyes, my fists clench, and my heart... my heart fucking aches at the sight before me.

The group of paintings is titled 'A World with Hope'. Hope, is the name we gave our baby. The series begins with her birth, and a cry wants to escape my chest at the sight of our sweet girl cradled in Tatum's arms as she was after she gave birth to her. A birth where we knew what the end result would be. Each cry and scream of Tatum's during labor was a mixture of pain and devastation at what was to come. Wrapped around both of them, are my own arms. A painful moment carved into my brain is made simply extraordinary through her eyes.

Next are a series of what should have been. Hope as a happy baby, grabbing her own toes with accomplishment in her eyes and what you can imagine is laughter bubbling from her lips. Hope as a toddler, looking unsteady as she walks toward hands reaching out to her. Hope, a look of unbridled glee on her face as she flies through the air while being pushed on a swing, wind blowing little wisps of her hair across her cheeks. Hope, eating an ice cream with chocolate smeared all over her face. The last piece is Hope, at the age she would be now, excitement in her eyes as she waits to get onto a school bus. All of the paintings take my breath away, bring tears to my eyes, and make my heart ache. But they also bring me a sliver of hope, because in the paintings where Hope is walking toward open arms and the other where she's being pushed on a swing, there are a man's hands present. This wouldn't be significant to anyone else, but to me, it's everything. Because, the man has a tattoo on the inside of his wrist, that matches the one on the inside of mine.

People around me are murmuring and commenting on how lovely the paintings are, how sweet. As a woman with a nametag stating she's gallery staff walks by I grab her lightly on the elbow, "Excuse me, is there a price list for the paintings? Specifically, these?" I don't care about my plan to save every last cent so I'm never dependent on anyone again. I will spend every last dime I have on these paintings.

"There is, but these are actually not for sale. They are the featured paintings she's sharing on her tour."

"Her tour?"

"Yes, she's visiting several galleries aside from this one."

Nodding I murmur, "Thank you."

After she walks away, I pull out my phone and take photos of the paintings. I don't know if it's allowed, but I don't care. Turning, I look around the room once more and still not finding Tatum, decide that I'm not meant to see her. That once was enough because it was more than I ever thought I would have. Besides, it may be for the best because I'm not sure my heart can handle once more.

Working my way through the crowd, I make my way to the door. A group of new comers walk inside and as they clear my path, I look up just as Tatum turns around from grabbing a glass of champagne from a waiter's tray, and locks eyes with mine. We stand frozen, both of us looking at the other, unable to look away, unable to take a step toward each other. So many things come to my mind, so many things I want to say, things I want to do. She looks simply...stunning.

Her eyes are bright and just as beautiful as I remember. I know dick about fashion, but I know that the short dress she's wearing was made for her. It hugs her curves perfectly and displays those long legs I love. My thoughts range from taking hold of her and kissing her, just wanting to feel her lips against mine again, to running my hand up her smooth leg and under her dress. My reaction to her is visceral, stronger than it was all those years ago.

But she's no longer mine. And the gap between the two of us is one that will never close. It's enough, more than enough, just to have had her beautiful eyes on mine again, however brief. With a small smile and a nod of my head, I quickly move out the door.

I've barely taken a few steps down the street toward home when the skies erupt with a fierce booming crash, seeming to echo the emotional turbulence churning within me. I pause, gaze toward the heavens, and as if on cue, rain begins to fall in a torrential downpour. It's as if God and all of his angels weep for me and Tatum...and our sad, broken love story.

CHAPTER FOUR

Tatum

These last five years have been ridiculously kind to him. He looks even better now than he did all those years ago when I first met him. An image of the day he came to pick up my roommate for a date comes to mind. I remember my instant draw to him and how I fought to push the strange feelings I was having away. My sarcastic comments, my emotions bouncing between annoyed and intrigued. Then there were the interactions that came after that, him asking me out on a date – repeatedly. My refusal every time and his unwillingness to accept "no" for an answer.

He looks… manlier I guess I would say. His build is bulkier, his muscles more defined even through his clothes. His beautiful face has even changed some. When he smiles, there are crinkles in the corners I don't remember being there before. My fingers twitch with a need to explore them, as well as the small dimple in his chin. But his eyes… his eyes are still the same, and the pull they had on me five years ago… it's still there.

My heart is racing, my breaths come quickly, and my stomach has a flock of damn birds inside. Part of me, a big part, wants to go to him. I suddenly find myself longing to hug him, kiss him, have him hold me in his arms like he used to. I have so many questions I'd like to ask him about the last five years. What has he been doing? Has he thought about me…missed me? Is he…with someone? Is he happy?

But another part of me, and it's just as big, wants to walk up to him and smack him on the face. I want to put my finger in his face and tell him I can't believe he'd show his face here. To scream, rant and rage. To scrape my nails down his face and make him feel the same pain he caused me. While my hand clenches tightly around my champagne glass, I honestly can't decide which act I'd prefer.

Somehow I manage to take a deep breath and control myself. I've moved on - I'm happy with Blaine. Those things are in the past. We were young and in pain and it was only a matter of time until we combusted. None of that changes the fact that we had many happy moments together, and regardless of our painful past, I will always care about him. Remember him. Miss him. Wonder what could have been, or should have been. Love him? I push that thought away and tell myself it's okay, he is the father of my baby.

Before I can make a move, he blesses me with a soft sad smile, and his eyes, full of many indecipherable emotions are still on mine. Then, he gives me a nod and before I can blink disappears into the crowd and moves toward the door.

Initially, I don't move. A million thoughts run through my mind at a speed so quick, it makes them impossible to catch and decipher. Before I can think twice, I'm pushing through guests offering "excuse me's", abandon my glass on a random table, and am out the door. Looking first to the right, the wind blows my hair straight into my face. I shove it aside, and frantically search the sidewalk for him, but I don't see anyone that resembles his physique. Rain is pouring down, and fortunately the awning is covering me, but it's hindering my vision. Looking to the left, I search the street of running rain dodgers and see a figure moving down the street, slower than one would expect given the weather. I know without a doubt, it's him. Some things you just don't forget.

"Cole!" I yell while at the same time wondering what I'm doing. Do I really want to come face to face with him? "Cole!" I yell again, I guess answering my own question. My voice is swallowed up in the sound of the weeping sky. With one look back at the gallery, hesitating momentarily, I turn and dart out into the rain.

Muttering a curse when the cold water hits my skin, I run toward him as fast as my heels will allow on the slippery sidewalk. "Cole," I yell again and this time he stops.

He stands still for a moment so I repeat his name once more.

He spins around and his eyes look around at a few other people and the area until they land on mine. Involuntarily gasping at the impact, it occurs to me that I never thought I would look into his eyes again. Eyes so dark, they're almost black, they've stayed with me all this time, and seeing them again feels heavy on my heart. Tears burn behind my eyes, but I ignore them and move toward him.

Arms wrapped around myself trying to fend off the cold, I hit a slippery patch on the sidewalk and curse internally knowing I'm going down. "Dammit."

Before my body reaches the ground, strong hands are there holding me steady. "Jesus," he mutters before he pushes me back against a closed store window, protecting me under an awning where the rain ceases to beat against my body.

For a moment we simply stare at each other. I'm soaked through, my hair hanging in strings down my face, the white part of my black and white cocktail dress now likely see through, and I'm sure my makeup is a mess. I'm almost angry at the fact that he manages to look so good. Sure his hair is plastered to his face, but he looks good wet. Not a mess like me. He's simply… stunning.

"Tatum?" he says my name under his breath and I watch as his eyes seem to devour my face. The combination makes a shiver run down my arms - it's been so long since I've heard him speak my name. Funny how such a simple thing, my name coming from his lips, could bring such immediate response. I shiver again and tighten my arms around myself. He notices and without speaking a word, he takes his suit jacket off and places it around my shoulders. Somehow there's still warmth inside and I revel in knowing it came from his body.

"Thank you," I tell him and feeling suddenly shy I look at the ground to gather myself. I'm not sure how to define exactly what I'm feeling, nor do I really know what I want to say now that he's right in front of me after so long. With a sigh, I shake it off and look into his eyes once more and ask the question at the forefront of my mind. "What are you doing here?"

He breaks eye contact and looks to the side. Before his eyes meet mine once more a smile graces his lips and he shrugs, "I came across a flyer for your show. I just…had to come."

He almost looks shy, his eyes silently wondering if his response will be satisfactory. "But why?"

"Why?" he repeats. "What do you mean?"

"Why would you want to come to my showing?"

His brows raise and lines crease his forehead in confusion, "To see you of course. Why else?"

"And so…what? You came, you saw, and you were just going to leave? Without even saying a word to me?"

"Seeing you needed to be enough – whether I like it or not. Besides, I didn't expect you to even see me."

"But, I did."

"Yes, and I'm sorry. I didn't mean to…" he trails off at a clear loss for words. He runs his hand through his wet hair. "I didn't think that far I guess. And if I had, I wouldn't have thought you'd be interested in even speaking to me. So, I wasn't intending on putting you in an uncomfortable position."

I almost want to laugh at his words, this whole interaction is uncomfortable, but his eyes are intense and they make me feel at a loss for words. There's a piece of me screaming inside telling me to just walk away. Don't do this to myself again. Don't care. Don't engage. Don't get invested. Just don't. Instead, I find myself nodding at his comment and we stare at each other, unsaid words and emotions passing through our eyes yet unable to do the same from our lips.

"You look," he begins and I almost jump at the sound of his voice. He eyes me up and down, and the way they scan my body is so intense I immediately feel transparent, vulnerable. A feeling I'm not sure I'd like to define crawls over my skin as his gaze brushes each part of me. "Amazing," he finishes.

"You too," I confess making sure I keep my eyes only on his.

We stare at each other and he blurts, "Are you happy?"

I open my mouth to respond, but find that 'yes' doesn't immediately come from my lips and it confuses me. I quickly and silently assess my life. I think about living in Chicago, a place I always wanted to go. I think about Blaine and our relationship over the last year. I think about my very first art showing here and how proud I feel inside. How I still love to lose myself in my paintings and haven't lost a passion for my work. But then I dig a little deeper into each of those things and I think about how much I didn't realize I miss Arizona. I wonder why I'm not happier with Blaine and my confusion over my feelings. I ponder my lack of good friends, other than my sister, and my longing for friends like I used to have when I lived here. I think about my paintings and how much I love my work, but there have been times more and more often where I'm experiencing intense block and I'm not sure where it's coming from. When it's quiet and I'm alone and I take time for self-reflection and dig deep, there's a feeling of something more… but it's beyond my scope. It's unattainable for me, but I have a desire to make whatever it is mine. But, I don't voice any of that. I just nod and give him a little smile.

"Good," he says looking away. I can see his jaw tightening as if he wants to say something but is forcing the words to remain unspoken.

Finally, I jerk my thumb in the direction of the gallery, "Well, I need to get back."

He clears his throat and straightens, "Yeah, of course. It was really good to see you."

"You too." We smile at each other a little while I remove his jacket and hand it to him and I consider hugging him or something, but chicken out and begin walking away instead after a little wave. After a few steps, I look over my shoulder and find he's still standing there, looking down at the ground. I take another couple steps, my heart seeming to ache at the growing distance. I look again and he's hooked his jacket over his shoulder and is slowly making his way down the sidewalk in the other direction.

Taking a deep breath, I look back in the direction of the gallery and begin walking again. I'm not sure the thought fully penetrates my mind before I'm twirling around again and almost jump when I find he's walking quickly toward me and is closer than I thought. When I'm facing him, his eyes widen a little and he stops. We smile hesitantly and I say, "Did you…"

"Would you…" he says at the same time and we laugh softly. "You first," he says and I swear there is something that looks like hope on his face.

"Oh, um, did you want to get coffee or something?"

He closes the distance between us, "Yes, I was going to ask you the same thing. I'm just not sure how long you're here?"

Avoiding that question for now, I ask, "Can you meet me in an hour? I need to get back to the gallery first, but the showing is almost over."

"That works. Do you remember where Nadine's is on Mill and University?"

"Yes," I nod, "I remember." We spent a lot of time studying at that coffee shop and I smile at the memory. He smiles too and I'm sure he's remembering the same thing. "I'll see you in an hour."

"Okay, see you there."

"Okay," I add and turn and head back to the gallery wondering what the hell I'm thinking.

An hour and a half later, I pull up in front of Nadine's. Closing out the showing took a little longer than I thought. I didn't have to stay to see everyone out, but it didn't feel right to leave before the last person left. Then when I finally got to my car to head over, Blaine called during his flight layover to see how the rest of the evening went. He had taken a flight back earlier tonight as we had planned, so he was only able to capture the beginning of the event. I recall my feeling irritated by the fact he couldn't stay, but now, a feeling of relief for his absence accosts me, but I quickly dismiss it.

Rather, I quickly reflect on the events after returning to the gallery. In honesty, I was rather impatient when I returned. Each question and kind comment from potential customers almost felt like an irritant instead of a compliment because I felt anxious to get back to Cole. The conflict was annoying and irritating, resulting in an internal battle from which there was no clear victor. Now that I'm late, I don't even know if he will still be here. He probably thought I decided not to come. It isn't like I could call him; I don't have his phone number any longer. At least, I assume I don't.

Shutting off my car's engine with a quick turn of the key, I take a moment to gather myself. Rubbing my temples I wonder what I'm even doing here? What we had was years ago, and while I can look on it now and chalk everything up to being young and broken, the issues themselves remain unresolved in a sense. There are so many things I don't understand, and in order to move on I had told myself I may never understand them, and that was okay. This could easily turn into something unpleasant if I let it, so I will ensure that does not happen. What does it have to do with today? With right now? Right? Besides, something inside of me couldn't stay away even if I tried. Maybe this will end up being the closure we weren't able to give each other before.

Pushing through the door I scan the room and feel relief when my eyes meet his. I smile at him apologetically, and walk to the table. He's already ordered a carafe of coffee and a mug awaits me. "I'm so sorry. It took longer than I thought it would to get out of there."

Fortunately, I had a change of clothes with me at the gallery. I quickly changed and used the bathroom hand dryer to do the best I could for my hair after retouching my make-up upon my return and am grateful that I stand here, no longer soaked to the bone. I see he's changed as well. His black shirt is rolled up at his forearms, tattoos trailing down his exposed skin. My eyes can't help but try to decipher the new additions since I've seen him last.

"It's okay. I understand."

After I pour my cup of coffee, I hold it between my hands enjoying the warmth while feeling at a loss for what to say. "So…" I say.

"So…" he repeats with a smile on his lips that makes my stomach flip. "How have you been?" he asks and it's so lame that I laugh. He laughs too and maybe doing so eases the tension a little. At least, my shoulders relax some.

"Well, I've been good," I tell him with a shrug.

"That's it? Five years and all I get is, 'I've been good'?"

"What would you like to know?"

He looks away from me for a moment before answering, "Given the art exhibition I'm assuming that means you finished art school with flying colors?"

"I did. As you know since I was only attending school part time my junior year here, I had some catching up to do once I arrived in Chicago." I clear my throat and push past the memories that bubble up mentioning that time. "They couldn't transfer all of my credits like they originally thought as well so I basically redid my junior year, went my senior year, and then decided to go on to graduate school for two years. I was lucky enough to maintain a full ride scholarship through it all, although at times, I'm not sure how."

He stares at me intently, "I'm sure the scholarship was a big help."

"It definitely took a lot of stress off, that's for sure. It included room and board and even a stipend for food. It was amazing really. I was very lucky."

"No, it's because of your talent and hard work, no doubt." I shrug and feel shy at his compliment. "So you graduated a year ago?"

"I did."

"Impressive that you have your own gallery tour just a year out of school." There's a look of pride on his face that feels intimate.

"I'd like to tell you it's all because of that talent and hard work you just mentioned, but it isn't."

"What do you mean?"

"I have the tour because I know people who know people. It's likely not something I'd have obtained on my own."

"Don't do that," he says, a stern look on his face and I look at him in confusion and a little insulted by his admonition. "Don't dismiss yourself, your talent, or your abilities so easily."

"Well, thank you." Deciding to move the conversation away from me, I decide I'd like some answers as well. "And you? You're doing well? What are you doing for a living? Did you go back to school full time and graduate?" Even though he was fighting on a scholarship in college, he still chose a major of course, which was accounting. He had plans to take his CPA exam to become a certified public accountant. He had hoped to get a job at a major accounting firm and eventually become a partner somewhere to support our family. That of course was then.

"I did not end up going back to college actually."

"No?"

"No. I'm fighting full time."

"Oh, wow. I guess I shouldn't be surprised. You were never able to stay out of the octagon. You loved fighting." He smiles a little, but doesn't respond. "So, it's going well then?"

"I do okay." He doesn't expand on that at all. Apparently Cole has become a man of few words. So, I push on, "And the guys? Are they all still fighting too?"

That generates the first full-blown smile I've seen on him in five years and the sight pulls at something within me leaving me momentarily breathless. A smile on Cole Russell can make young women's panties drop, babies giggle, and even elderly women look his way. It affects *all* the ladies.

"They are – every one of them. I'm sure you remember Jax, Zane, Levi, Dylan, and Ryder from college."

"I don't think any woman in her right mind could forget any of you."

"Is that right?"

"It is."

"So does that mean that you never forgot about me?"

CHAPTER FIVE

Cole

It takes everything I have to sit here and keep to myself. I want to touch her, to move to the other side of the table, sit next to her, take her hands in mine. I want to tell her how much I've missed her. That I think about her all the time, that I never forgot her, could never replace her, even when I wanted to so damn much in my efforts to block thoughts of her.

Being this close to her and not able to act on my feelings is the worst kind of torture. I do my best to maintain a normal conversation, but I'm pretty sure I sound like a robotic asshole.

I wait for her to answer my question. I shouldn't have asked it, I know, but it was out of my mouth before I could shove the words back. The tops of her cheeks flush pink and I can see her struggle for words. I want to hear her answer in the affirmative so desperately. I clutch my hands into fists trying to reign in my emotions. When she doesn't say anything, and I can't take any more of the awkward silence, I laugh, as if I was only joking and change the subject with a new question. "How are your parents doing, and your sister?"

Her shoulders relax and I feel a mixture of disappointment and frustration that she was clearly bothered by my asking her if she thought about me. "They're good. Mom and dad retired to Florida a couple years ago. They love it there, and I try to visit whenever I can. Teagan is still in California. In fact, I have a gallery showing there in a few weeks. My mom and dad will be flying in for it and staying with her. I'm really looking forward to seeing all of them – it's been awhile. Mom and dad wanted to try to come to this one initially, but California works best so they can see both of us. How's your mom?"

"She's fine. Still lives in here in Arizona, and is always busting my balls over one thing or another."

"I'm not surprised one bit," she says with a smile. She and my mom had been extremely close. We used to spend a lot of time at my house back then. Partly because my mom worked a lot and before we lived together, it was a place we could go to have some alone time. It was also because she and my mom genuinely loved one another. I ruined that when I basically sent Tatum away. My mom wouldn't speak to me for weeks afterward. She kept asking questions in order to understand what had happened, but I refused to speak of it. Besides, I couldn't tell anyone anyway. Another part of the agreement.

"Yeah, you shouldn't be. She's a woman of tradition if nothing else. She's still a pain in my ass."

"Oh please, you love your mom. You always were a mama's boy," she teases and the tone of her voice and smile on her face take me away to another time. A time when teasing and flirting with one another eventually led to touching and kissing. God, I have missed her. I feel like a thirteen-year-old girl with all of these prissy emotions running through me.

"Guilty," I give in easily to her teasing.

"Does she still randomly stop by your home with enough food to feed an army?"

"Not my place anymore, no. She stops in at the gym and hands out food to all the guys and me. It actually pisses me off to be honest. I can't tell you how many times I've fought with Levi over her sugar cookies, and Ryder acts like any time she brings in pasta it's especially for him."

She laughs, "Well tell her to quit."

"Are you kidding? I wouldn't dream of it, she loves the attention. I'll sacrifice my stomach for her self-esteem I suppose."

"Aw, you're such a martyr."

I chuckle and shrug not denying it while I look at her over the brim of my coffee mug as I take a sip. I can't help but stare at her. Her long dark hair frames her face and is now curling a bit due to standing in the rain earlier. Her blue green eyes, framed by dark lashes, sparkle in this lighting. They are as bright and expressive as I remember. Her lips, the top a little thinner than the fuller bottom have always made it look like she's pouting just a little in an unbelievably sexy way. She's dressed casually in a blue shirt and jeans, but the shape of her body is clear underneath. I have no doubt if I close my eyes I would remember what it feels like to touch her skin. I remember every curve, divot and line vividly.

Beautiful pale skin, need in her eyes, want and desire coming from her lips during our naked moments. And then I remember last night - seeing her through the glass of the gallery. Smiling at a man, kissing him. The images in my mind fade and my hands clench into fists once more as I casually place them under the table. I want to ask her about him, demand to know who he is, how she met him, how serious they are, but I don't. The questions remain on the tip of my tongue, but unasked.

"How are you liking Chicago?" I ask her as a way to push the unwanted thoughts from my mind.

"It's good. I love the city, I mean is there any better skyline, theater, live music, or shopping anywhere else? The variety of restaurants has practically turned me into a foodie - but you know, it's city living," she shrugs and smiles as if I should know what she means. I've never been out of Arizona a day in my life. She pauses, takes a deep breath and continues. "I live in a great area, not far from the lakeshore – so I'm lucky in that way, of course. I'm able to walk everywhere, don't even own a car. But everyone is in a hurry whether they are walking on the street or driving. And the winter's, oh my god, don't even get me started. The wind just goes right through you."

I nod and try to soak in every word she's saying but I find myself distracted. I think I'm only catching the highlights, the *USA Today* version. Watching her takes over listening. As she talks, her hands move. She gestures constantly, but when she laughs or gets excited about something her gestures become bigger mimicking her tone. When she struggles to remember a detail, she looks up as if it helps her recall them better. When she's shy or embarrassed, she bites her lip and looks down. She's a hair tucker too, always pushing it out of her face and behind her right ear. When she's nervous, she still bites her lip or picks her nails. I remember teasing her because there were times she would have just painted her nails and then already be scratching the color off. And her laugh, god, how could I have forgotten how it sounds? Such a girly giggle that makes my own lips twitch with the need to smile or laugh with her. I've forgotten so many things. Things I promised myself I would never forget. Could never forget. And I don't know whether to hate myself for it or to be thankful that I forgot them, because it would only have hurt more to be able to easily recall them all this time.

She's mesmerizing, like a song that makes your heart pound faster and your body pulse with the need to dance. I'm basking in her presence, knowing our time is limited and wanting to memorize everything about her once more.

"You would love it," she says, and I have no idea what she's talking about. I must look at her blankly because she says, "You'd love how green everything is. And how in the Fall everything changes colors and creates the most beautiful landscape that I can't come close to replicating in my paintings no matter how hard I try."

"Sorry, but I'm going to have to disagree with you. I've seen your paintings. I doubt there's anything that you can't capture in your paintings."

"You're just being kind, but thank you."

"No, I'm telling you the truth." She nods, but a cloud crosses her eyes with my words and she seems to retreat a little. I'd give anything to know what is going on in her mind right this second.

We sit in silence for a moment as we each drink our coffees and I struggle for a question to ask or anything to say that will keep our conversation going. Something, anything, that isn't loaded with all of the unsaid words between us.

And then I fail, because I choose to go there anyway. "Speaking of your paintings…" I pause, not sure how to proceed now that I've already opened my mouth.

Her brow furrows and her eyes search my face as if she's trying to pluck the words from my mind before I say them, "Yes?"

My thoughts are so jumbled up with my emotions, untangling them all to try and ask a coherent question is difficult. "I…when I was at the showing…" she nods and watches me watch her. "I saw them." Before I say anything else, her face stills and I watch closely for something that betrays what she's thinking - what she's feeling. She gives away nothing, her face a blank canvas, waiting for me to paint it with words before she betrays their definitions in color. "I saw the paintings of Hope."

She nods, still not saying anything. Her throat moves as she swallows, then reaches for her mug and takes a drink of her lukewarm coffee. Finally, she nods, "I wondered if you had."

"I'd like to buy them."

"Buy them?"

"Yes," I nod. "All of them."

She looks at me then looks to the side and back at me again. She starts scratching at her fingernails and I can't help myself, I reach out and take her hand in mine. She swallows and shakes her head, "They aren't for sale."

"That's what they said when I asked, but I was hoping maybe I could convince you to sell them to me."

She pulls her hand away from mine and I feel its absence immediately. "Why?"

"Why, what?"

"Why do you want them?"

"What kind of question is that?" I feel confusion and a few embers of anger start smoldering in my stomach. How can she even ask me that?

"It's a valid question, but it doesn't matter because like I said, they are not for sale."

"Okay, then can I convince you to paint copies for me? It doesn't even have to be all of them. I'll take just one. Whichever one you can do."

She stands abruptly and her cup of coffee falls over with a clatter, the little contents left splashing on the table top. She grabs her purse and when she starts to make her way to the door, I'm so shocked and confused it takes me a few beats before I run after her.

Once out the door, I look right and left before I see her stalking to a black car. Running to her, I grab her arm and turn her to face me, "Tatum, what the hell?"

"Why do you even care, Cole?"

It's as if she's smacked me. My head snaps back with the viciousness of her words and I'm instantly angry, "Excuse me?"

"Why are you acting like you give a fuck? I don't understand any of this." And she gestures wildly and I know she's talking about my showing up at the gallery, our coffee, my request, everything.

"How can you say that to me?"

"It's simple, I move my mouth and the words come out."

"I'm serious, Tatum." I reply sternly not finding her sarcasm amusing in the slightest.

"It doesn't matter. This was a mistake. All of it was a mistake."

I let go of her as if she's burned my hand with her words. I watch helplessly as she searches her purse frantically for the keys to her car and I feel frantic at the thought of her walking away again. Not like this. Not again. Placing my hand on the door, alongside her head, I plead, "Tatum, please. Don't go."

She turns to look at me, and I'm gutted by the tears in her eyes. "I can't do this, Cole. I thought I could, but I can't. I've moved on. I'm happy. But this," she gestures between the two of us, "this still hurts and I'm not willing to take a knife to my scars and reopen what has been healing and allow them to bleed anymore. I've come too far to take steps back to that painful time, and that's what you are. I can pretend all I want but that's what you are - pain."

Finding her keys, I hear a sigh of relief leave her as she presses the button to unlock the door. She gets inside and I grab hold of the door before she can close it. She hangs her head for a moment before looking up at me, "Goodbye, Cole." She closes the door, starts the car and leaves taking my heart and soul with her once again.

"Goodbye, Tatum."

CHAPTER SIX

Tatum

It's been a long time since I've cried myself to sleep, but as soon as my eyes open in the morning, I remember doing so the night before. After returning to my hotel room, I collapsed into bed without even changing my clothes, brushing my teeth, or removing my makeup. I let the emotions from the day and memories from long ago chase me into sleep.

Groaning, I roll away from the sunlight brazenly blasting through the curtains I neglected to close last night. Grabbing the pillow beside me, I shove it over my face briefly hoping I can fall back asleep, but all at once it hits me. I remember what day it is and what it means to me. It's why I almost didn't agree to my showing being so close to this day, but then decided maybe a short stay here is long overdue, and just maybe exactly what I need.

Slowly getting out of bed, I find myself in the bathroom staring at my reflection in the mirror. Standing calmly my eyes trace the lines of my face and then I look into my own eyes, trying to see it. I know it's there, but yet on the surface my look is deceiving. The vision presented is an average woman with dark hair, a straight nose that lifts slightly at the tip, a few freckles across the bridge, a small dimple in my chin and high cheekbones some women have told me they'd kill to have themselves. Staring harder, I look for it again until my eyes begin to water. For a moment, I feel proud of the façade I've worked hard to place there. I wear the mask well. Some days it's even genuine – I feel happy, fulfilled even though not in the way I'd hoped or expected, but some days, some moments, it's enough.

I think if one of my friends was ever asked , "What's Tatum like?" they would say I'm a confident woman that's comfortable with her early success as an artist. That I'm happy with my life, shy at times, but kind and giving and that I seem happy with my life, boyfriend and my home. I think they would say I'm a hard worker, smart, and that I've worked hard to be where I am, that I earned it. I've made sure to be that woman at least, because those things matter, but those attributes also help hide the truth that I prefer to keep private.

Closing my eyes, I let go. I imagine pouring water over the top of my head; it falls down my face in rivers, slides down my neck and drips down my body. As it falls, it erases the paint of deception that the truth hides behind. This time, when I open my eyes and look in the mirror, it's there. I can see it now. The brokenness. The sorrow. The grief.

I'm a broken mirror – one that dropped and shattered into pieces. Over the years I've begun the painstakingly slow process of gluing myself back together, but the triumphs haven't come without blood dripping splinters and slices. Therapy has helped; eventually I was able to move forward easier, I found the beauty in things again. My faith, my hopes, my dreams, they were all things that I was able to rediscover and helped put the pieces in place once more. But, as is the way with putting something broken back together, the pieces never quite fit the same way again. Some of the pieces that went together so perfectly at one time, no longer have a place – some are forever broken, others are missing.

No one would guess that my pain was once so deep and vast that getting out of bed, participating in the most mundane activities and simply surviving took an incredible amount of strength, thought, motivation and work. I still feel that pain at times, still wish my life had gone a different direction, find myself dreaming about what could have been, but I long since learned that those kinds of thoughts get me nowhere. That those pieces, they just fit differently now and that I have to be okay with that. I'm not the same person I used to be. Dreams change. Wishes change. I've worked hard to move past those times. To no longer be a shadow of myself but to somehow stand in the light again. And some times... some times I feel like I'm close - so close. But, I'm not where I would like to be - not yet. I can still see those broken pieces far too easily when I let down my guard, when I speak honesty to myself and allow my true self to briefly emerge. Maybe I've just not adjusted to this new me. Maybe the broken pieces are just a part of my new self. Perhaps it will always be this way, but I'd like to think that someday, somehow, in some way, I'll only have a crack left, no more pieces. And when I look, I will see a me that is complete – whole, unfractured.

Except for days like today. Days like today, there's no hope of that.

Disrobing, I wait for the water to warm and then step into the shower. Closing my eyes at the feel of the warmth against my skin, I slide down the side of the shower wall and sit on the floor. Placing my head in my hands, I finally allow my thoughts to go where they really want. Taking a deep breath to prepare myself, as I exhale, I open the little box I keep locked up tight, and I let myself remember.

I remember the surprise, nervousness and excitement of finding out that I was pregnant. I remember that while I was afraid of the changes to my life that a baby would incur, that the words from the doctor's mouth still made me feel awe at the miracle of creating life. I let myself remember the anticipation I felt at meeting the small person inside of me. I allow myself to recall the look on Cole's face when I told him about our creation. I can still see the look on his face when he saw our baby for the first time on the monitor during an ultrasound, heard her heartbeat for the first time, and when we found out we were having a girl. I remember the surprised wonder on his face when he felt her move for the first time. Tears mix with water and run down my face as I recall the whispered dreams for our child we shared in each other's arms at night. How we imagined how she would look and how we laughed and vetoed various baby name suggestions, never quite finding the perfect name until… until after she was here.

Running my hands through my hair, I rest my head on my knees as memories of the night I lost my child go through my mind. How frightened I was knowing something was wrong and feeling helpless to be able to do anything about it. My refusal to believe the worst. My scream when they told me the baby I had just felt moving hours before, no longer stirred with life. The agony of having to go through the motions of child birth knowing that in the end there wouldn't be happy tears and celebration. My heart tears in two and the sobs come as I remember finally holding her in my arms. She was so tiny, yet still absolute perfection. Counting her ten fingers and ten toes, touching the tiny wisps of hair on her head, running my finger over her tiny cheek. Kissing the tip of her nose that looked just like mine. Wishing with all of my heart that I could see what her eyes looked like as they stared into my own. Seeing a whole lifetime of wishes and dreams that I had for my child flash before my eyes in an instant. My initial refusal to let her go until Cole put his hands on my own and looked into my eyes, his pain reflecting my own. Holding his arms out, he took her from me and held her too. I watched riveted as his eyes devoured our baby girl and tears fell down his face.

Rubbing my hands hard over my face, I do my best to push past those memories and think of the ones that make me smile. I imagine what she would look like now, today, on what would have been her fifth birthday.

Her hair is dark like mine, and her eyes are dark like Cole's. Her smile would light up a room and people would turn to look or smile if they heard her laugh ring out amongst them. She'd be incredibly bright and inquisitive asking "why" for everything, I'm sure. She would make me laugh, make it hard to be stern with her, and she would have a sensitive and kind heart. She would be the light of my life – she wouldn't be an imagined painting. She'd be real – flesh and blood. I could hold her, kiss her, tell her how much I love her every single day.

Somehow I find comfort knowing that my little girl is in heaven, with a full heart knowing how much she's loved. I used to want to do anything to be there with her, but I finally found honor and purpose in living for her instead. It took me a long time to get to that point - to heal. I still have difficult moments, but they don't take me to the edge of despair like they used to. Feeling pain and recalling the desire I once had to give into it no longer makes me think myself weak. Through my pain I found within myself true strength, courage, and determination at continuing to take steps forward.

Rising to my feet, I take a big breath, and choose to move forward now. Grabbing the shampoo, I pour a handful and while washing my hair my thoughts eventually turn to seeing Cole last night. I couldn't wrap my mind around why Cole would want a painting of Hope. I don't know why it appeared to matter so much to him. It isn't that I don't think he mourned the loss of our daughter, I know he did in his own way. I clearly remember the sadness and despair in his eyes, but I also remember he found his way through our loss much quicker than I did. He would seem exasperated when I held onto my grief longer than he would like, than he was comfortable with. I can easily recall the way his jaw would clench and his fists would tighten when he'd find me in bed hours after he had left me there in the morning. There were many times I saw him run his hands through his hair in exasperation, his words begging me to get up, to go for a walk, to go to work, to make myself something to eat…anything. I know now through therapy that I had a nasty case of post partum depression, something I, nor Cole, realized. It didn't even occur to me that I could suffer from it considering I didn't have a baby in my arms to prove I deserved the diagnosis. Still, in my mind it seemed like I cared about our loss a whole hell lot more than Cole. Over the years, considering how we left things, I determined it was simply that he was able to let go and move on faster and easier than I. Maybe it was because he didn't have her inside of him, didn't feel her move as often, didn't feel as if his life had been blended with hers yet. I don't know. I really don't. While I'm in a better place now certainly, the child I lost will forever be a part of me. There isn't a day that goes by that I don't think of her in some way. She's a piece of me, one of the best parts, and while she my not be here, I'm still her mother. I am still a mother.

Then, as if things aren't complicated enough, I also feel guilty for my self righteous feelings toward Cole. Who the hell am I to decide what Cole has a right to feel and not feel, and moreover when or how or with whom he feels it? The fact is, I don't know how he feels about Hope, or what he thinks about when he looks back on that time. I do know that clearly my paintings affected him. I know that when he looked at me last night, I could see and feel his regret, his sorrow. I also know that when I saw him, something within me shifted – I don't know why, or how, or what it means, but I wanted, no needed, to talk to him, to hear how he is, and to see for myself that he's doing well.

I let my emotions get the best of me perhaps and I feel a little guilty that I took off the way that I did. It isn't how I would have preferred to say goodbye to him, but it's for the best I think. What else do we have to say to each other? What good will it do to rehash anything? He made his choice long ago.

Stepping out of the shower I make quick work of getting myself ready. It isn't long before I'm out the door of my hotel and on my way. After a quick stop, I pull into a parking lot looking for a spot, my emotions feeling on the edge once more. When I get out of the rental car, I look up taking in the cloudy day. Overcast days are commodities in Arizona, there aren't always many. It seems as if the weather is just for me, mimicking my mood today.

After a short walk, I find myself looking down at the grave of my daughter. I choke on a sob and sink to my knees, my fingers immediately tracing the letters of her name. I haven't visited her grave in the five years she's been here. When I had the chance to move to Chicago, I almost didn't go, the thought of leaving Hope here was too much to bear. In the end, moving to Chicago seemed the least painful choice.

"Hi, baby girl," I whisper without meaning to and clear my throat. "It's your mommy." Running my hand over the top of her gravestone and around the base, I am surprised when there isn't debris to clear. The site appears well cared for, and I'm grateful for that. "I'm so, so, sorry that it's taken me so long to visit you. I hope you can forgive me." A couple tears escape despite my best effort to keep them at bay. It can't be helped I don't think. My heart feels like it's shriveling up in my chest and dying.

"I brought you some flowers. I stood in the store forever trying to decide what kind I should bring to you. It's hard you see, because I never got the chance to find out what your favorite color would be, or what your favorite flower would have been." I shake my head and another tear rolls down my cheek. "Such a simple choice for some people, completely overwhelming for me. I didn't want to choose wrong." I laugh without humor and wipe at my face. "So, you know what I did? I closed my eyes. I closed my eyes and I thought of you. I imagined what you would look like today. In my imagination you had on a pink dress and your dark hair is in pigtails, and in your arms, more flowers than you could hold. I could see the look on your face, baby, I could! I saw delight in your dark eyes at the bright color and the delightful smell. You looked up at me with a big smile, holding them out to me and when I looked down, they were yellow roses. I'm not sure why, but that's why I chose them. I hope it's okay." I place the flowers at the base of her grave, startled at the shock of color it presents against the dull gray of her stone and the drab green of Arizona's version of grass.

"I live in Chicago now. I received a scholarship out of the blue to an art school and decided to go. I didn't want to leave you, please know that, but I needed something…anything to help me put one foot in front to the other again, because losing you made living without you hard. It wasn't easy, believe me. But…but I hope that if you can look down on me, I hope that I've made you proud. That I'm the kind of mom that you would have loved to have." I continue my one-sided conversation, telling Hope all about my art, my paintings of her, and about my art show. I have no idea how long I talk to her, but I know that time passes considering the sun that was at my back before is now directly overhead. I could care less about how long I've been here though. Sitting here speaking to her feels comforting, something within me clicking into place, a need I didn't even know I had soothing my soul.

"You know, it occurs to me that I've never told you I'm sorry," I tell her, my voice breaking on the words. "I am, Hope. I am so, so sorry that I lost you. I've gone over and over it. I don't know what I did. I don't know why it happened. I'm not even sure what I could or should have done differently. All I know is that my body failed you, failed me. My therapist and doctor's have told me that this wasn't anything that I could control. They said that sometimes these things happen without rhyme or reason, or because something was wrong with the pregnancy in general. But, I know it's my fault. And believe me when I tell you that I live with that every single day. If I could go back and do it over and I don't know…stay in bed the whole time or something, I would in a moment. A second. I would give anything, anything at all to make the outcome different." The tears come heavy now, words I never intended to speak out loud streaming from my mouth as if saying them will deliver me from the shame I feel inside. "It's important to me that you know that I wanted you, more than anything. And that I love you. So much."

"And Hope, your daddy loved you too," I say fiercely, confident my words are more for me than for her. "We would have made great parents, I know it. If only we had been given the chance." I don't know why, but I begin speaking to her about my feelings about Cole. "I'm so mad at your dad sometimes. Other times I'm just...sad. I hate that discarding me and getting over this was easy for him. That he was able to move on with little regard for anything but himself. Must have been nice I guess." Sighing heavily, I pick a piece of grass and twirl it in my fingers, looking off into the sky. "I know we all deal with things in different ways, it's just that seeing him again has stirred up some emotions for me I suppose. It's hard when you realize someone you loved so much isn't who you thought he was."

"Are you fucking kidding me?" Cole's voice says angrily behind me making me cry out and stand up, turning to face him and when I do, I immediately take a step back and gasp at the look on his face.

CHAPTER SEVEN

Cole

When I woke up this morning, the first thing I did was get ready to visit Hope. I almost said something to Tatum when I saw her last night, had the crazy notion that maybe we could go together, but she left before I had the chance to bring it up. Upon arriving a few minutes ago, I saw her as soon as Hope's grave came into view. Seeing her sitting at our daughter's grave made my chest hurt and my eyes burn, and my memory flies back to the day we buried her, no service or anything, just us and close friends. I remember her head bowed, tears flowing down her cheeks, and how I had to practically carry her from the cemetery.

At first I try to give her space, I do, but the lure of her is too strong and before I realize what I'm doing, I find myself standing at her back. Listening as she apologizes to Hope almost brings me to my knees. She's so wrapped up in her words, she never hears me approach.

When she tells our daughter how much I love her, I smile sadly wishing I could tell her that myself – in person. When her words turn to anger, I can't believe what I'm hearing at first. On a rational level, I get that she's venting, and definitely isn't expecting me to overhear, but to know what she thinks and hear her suggest that anything about this has been easy for me, sets my blood on fire. She has no idea. No idea what I go through every day – for her. Where does she get the right to assume anything about me? It's more than I can take, and I can no longer remain silent, letting my anger be voiced. She spins around in surprise and one look at my face makes her eyes widen in surprise at being caught.

"Easy for me? How can you think that anything about this has been easy for me? Who the hell do you think you are?" I turn away from her and try to gather myself.

"I think I'm hitting the metaphorical bulls eye with that statement, that's what the hell I think." She says and I turn back around to find her surprised look replaced with fierce ire. "How can you expect that I would think anything else? Do you even remember that time, Cole? Because I remember; I remember it well."

"So, do I, *Tatum*," I say her name as harshly as she said mine, as if doing so gives the statement harsher emphasis. "I remember it all too. It's not as if I could forget. God, I remember how much it hurt," I choke out, running my hand through my hair and looking to the sky as if comfort can be found there. "It was like someone took my insides and twisted them around and around. It took months and months for me to unwind it all, little by little."

She laughs and my eyes snap back to her in disbelief. But she does it again. She fucking laughs and it takes everything I have to remain calm. I'd give anything to be at a gym or in a fight right now. I want to pound my fists against a sandbag in order to get this feeling out of me. "Oh my God," she clutches her stomach as if I've made the funniest joke she's ever heard. "That's rich. *You* were broken? *You* were hurt? You've got to be kidding me."

"Why? Are you the only one who had a right to feel grief or sorrow in all of this? If so, fuck you, Tatum, fuck you. Because I felt so much, so fucking much and you have no right to suggest I didn't." I look down, taking a breath to try to calm myself, but it doesn't work. Anger fills me so fast and so hard I'm dizzy with it. It's like I'm a gas tank and each look of disbelief, each laugh or denial in her eyes gives my anger more and more fuel. When I look back at her, I find her mouth open ready to say god knows what. I point a finger at her and she shakes her head and laughs again to herself and it's as if she lit a match. It sets me on fire. "I blamed myself," I say softly at first, but then, I scream it. I scream it so loud and so long, that it feels ridiculously satisfying. "I BLAMED MYSELF!"

The silence in the air feels shocking after such a loud outburst. It feels like I've always needed to scrape the words off of my heart and lay them bare - to say them aloud. "Do you get that? Did that even occur to you? God Tatum, for a long time, I hated myself for not being able to save her," I confess, quieter now. "To not be able to save you such complete and utter pain. I thought that maybe if I had gotten you to the hospital faster it would have saved her. Maybe if I had insisted you quit going to school and quit working, she would have been okay. Maybe if I had demanded we go to the doctor when you complained about back pain earlier in the day, it would have made all the difference. So many 'what if's', so many things I came up with that I should have done. Lists, Tatum, I made goddamn lists – on paper over and over - in my mind of all the ways I failed you both."

"You never said a word about it."

"Of course I didn't. I couldn't. I couldn't voice any of it. I couldn't say a thing. All I wanted was to hold you, cry with you, rant and rave at the world with you, and grieve together. Instead, I held it in. I kept it to myself because you-" I break off as a vision of her all those years ago flashes before my eyes, and I let myself remember.

I remember the vivid contrast of her dark hair against white sheets as she lay in bed for god knows how many hours. I remember the film of grief over her eyes, the gauntness in her cheeks, and the lack of will in her movements. I remember how she would sit and stare for hours at nothing. I remember how she would cry constantly, and nothing I said or did could soothe her. I let myself remember how certain days I had to beg her to get out of bed and I would leave the apartment to go to work and sit in my car and cry. I remember feeling helpless, and feeling scared when she would stare at nothing for hours and would refuse to eat. I remember promising God anything if he would just help me find a way to help her.

"You couldn't take on my pain too," I tell her honestly. "I couldn't do that to you, so instead I hid it the best way I could. I lied about it, and I tried to take care of you, but I didn't know what to do, or how to help you," I confess. "But, nothing ever seemed to help. Half the time I don't think you even knew I was there."

She walks up to me, and shakes her head. "So your solution was to get rid of me? The first solution that came along you jump on whole-heartedly and push me out?" Tears start to fall down her cheeks and she swipes at them in anger. "You wanted me gone," she says and then out of nowhere she pushes me hard. "You left me! You abandoned me!" she screams. "I may have been the one to physically pack and leave, but as soon as that scholarship came in, you couldn't wait to get me out of there. You left me emotionally, long before I moved away. It was like I was a broken piece of furniture that you decided you no longer wanted in your home. I was disposable."

"You're wrong," I state emphatically.

"How can you fucking say that?" she screams and pushes me again.

I stare at her for a minute and am consumed by her heaving breaths, red cheeks and watery eyes. Damn, she's beautiful. She takes my breath away. Always has and always will. And in seeing her more clearly, I instantly remember where we are, and what day it is and my anger tapers off and vanishes. "This isn't going to get us anywhere. We can't change things, and yelling at each other here and now isn't how I intended to spend my visit with Hope."

She stares at me with her arms crossed and says nothing. Moving past her, I finally set down the flowers I brought for my little girl at the base of her headstone. "Hi, sweet girl. I'm sorry it's been a few weeks since I've been here to see you. Things have been a bit busy, and the days have been getting away from me too fast. But, you know that I think about you every day." I touch the top of her stone and then bend down to pull a small weed from the corner placing it into my pocket to dispose of later. They do a great job keeping things looking nice here, but I take care of whatever they miss. "Happy Birthday, Hope. If you were here, I think your gift this year would have been a pink bike, or maybe blue, depending on your favorite color. I do know it would have had a huge basket on the front and I'm pretty sure a bell would be required. I bet you'd be a natural which means you'd be a speed demon and you'd need that bell to warn people out of your way." I smile at the thought and then trace my fingers over her name. "I love you. I'll be back soon."

Turning, keeping my head down, I decide it's past time to leave. Stopping when I'm side by side with Tatum, I don't look into her face, but tell her one last thing. "I know you don't believe it, and that's okay. But, I just want to say that I will never get over losing her, and I will *never* get over losing you."

With that, I begin walking to my car, picking up the pace the further I retreat from Hope's grave, eager to leave and have some time to myself to contemplate the words spoken here today.

"You were here a few weeks ago?" Her voice stops me and after a short pause, I turn around. Reluctantly meeting her eyes, I sigh, not wanting to argue any longer. She repeats herself, "Do you come here often?"

"As often as I can, yes."

"For the last five years?"

Nodding, I tell her honestly, "Every chance I get."

She looks away and I see tears fall down her cheeks again, "I don't understand you, Cole. I don't understand at all."

Walking to her, I hesitate, but then decide I have nothing to lose. I have to be careful, I can't tell her everything, but I will say what I can without jeopardizing anything. Taking the tops of her arms into my hands, I give them a slight squeeze. I half expect her to pull away, but she lifts her chin and her eyes that were staring at my chin before meet my own. "I know that it doesn't make sense to you. I get it. All I can say is that not everything is what it seems."

"What does that mean?"

"I can't say more than that."

"What the hell does that mean?" she asks again, frustration evident in her tone.

"You leaving…it broke me. It wasn't easy, but to me, it was the only way to save you."

"Maybe I didn't want to be saved."

"Yes you did."

"How do you know that?"

"We both know that, Tatum, now more than ever. Life…it can be taken so quickly, without warning, and so easily. Being alive, even when it seems to be the hardest choice of the two, is a gift. Choosing anything else, it's not an option, not when living for her," I nod toward Hope's grave, "and carrying her with us, is the only way that she can stay alive too."

Tears fall down her face non-stop now, but she nods and wipes them away. I find myself smiling at her and tucking a stray piece of hair behind her ear. "I'm sorry that I couldn't let myself show you my pain at your leaving. I was afraid that if I did, you wouldn't go. And you needed to go. Staying here, it wouldn't have helped you get well."

"You don't know that. We could have talked about it, found some other way."

I shake my head, knowing that there wasn't another way. The school, her art, it was the only thing that would have brought her the healing she needed. And in order for it to happen for her, she had to leave. That was the deal, like it or not. My wants and desires didn't matter, and besides, putting her needs first was easy. There was no other way. "There wasn't," I tell her.

"I don't understand," she says in confusion.

"I know. Just remember what I said, not everything is always the way it seems."

She sighs and I can see her irritation. I don't blame her. "It was…well…I am happy that I got to see you again," I tell her. "I think of you often and I'm glad that you are doing well." My hands fall from her arms and my fingers twitch with the need and desire to put them back.

"I'm glad I got to see you too."

Before I can think twice, I lean in and kiss her cheek. Moving back to look at her face, I brush my thumb over her cheek, then take a chance and lean in and place a kiss on her mouth. Her breath catches in surprise, but I linger there for a few seconds before pulling back and dropping my hands from her completely. With one last long look at her, I turn and walk away without another word knowing I need to be the one to do so this time around. I don't think I can handle watching her leave one more time.

I'm almost to the gate that leads to the parking lot when I hear her words ring out and they stop me in my tracks. "Cole! Wait! Please. Don't leave me. I don't… I don't want you to go."

CHAPTER EIGHT

Tatum

As soon as the words are out of my mouth I have a moment of wishing it were possible for me to snatch them out of the air and take them back. My mind is a carousel of thoughts; whirling so fast I can barely compute them all. One minute I'm angry at his lack of caring and the ease of which he was able to move on, and in the next I'm faced with a different reality. One in which he felt broken too, one where he suppressed his own emotions in order to take the best care of me. Where he tells me that things aren't what they seem. What does that even mean? Can I really not see him again without getting to the bottom of that comment? Is simply knowing there is more to it than meets the eye good enough or me? Hell no.

As if that's not enough, to find out he visits Hope routinely makes my heart ache with longing. Longing to jump into his arms so I can thank him for taking care of our girl. It may be something that may not seem like a big deal to some, but to me, it's everything. All these years I couldn't let myself think about the fact that she was here – alone. But she hasn't been. Not at all.

His back is to me and I have no doubt a gamut of expressions cross my face before he turns around to face me. I'm unsure of what I want here – the words poured from my mouth before I could give them definition. What I do know is that I don't want him to leave. The thought makes me feel like I can't breathe. Maybe it's because there's unfinished business between us. Maybe it's because I haven't seen him in so long and even after all this time, some part of me connects the essence of coming home to be defined as simply being in his presence. Or it could be nothing more than the fact that letting go is hard. With him, I think it always will be. I should probably just let him leave. It will hurt…it will feel like breaking my arm in a way, but while the pain will linger for a while, it will eventually disappear. It will heal.

He's staring at me, not saying a word. I open my mouth to tell him I'm crazy, that I don't know why I said that. To just forget it. By the look on his face I wonder if he even heard me correctly, but I'm sure as hell not going to say it again, even if he asks me to repeat myself. I find myself returning his stare, not moving, not speaking, just waiting to see what he does. When he begins walking toward me, I hold my breath. I'm afraid if I don't, he'll be able to tell how nervous I am.

When we're toe to toe, he asks, "How much longer will you be in Arizona?"

Not what I was expecting. Letting my breath out slowly, I take a moment to answer. "A few more days."

He nods and his jaw clenches as he looks away. I take the opportunity to devour his face. I admire his strong stubbly jaw, his chiseled cheekbones, and strong neck. My eyes quickly move over his body, unable to keep myself from checking out the changes since I last saw him. He's bigger now than before. His shoulders are broader; his muscles under his short sleeve shirt more defined. He's added artwork to his arms. I can't help but wonder if he's added work anywhere else too. Where are they located? What do they mean to him? When and why did he get them? My fingers twitch at the thought of tracing the designs and asking him.

He looks back at me and his eyes scan my face. "Would you…" His voice trails off and he appears to hesitate looking down at the ground before looking back at me. I wait a beat for him to finish his sentence, but he remains silent. "Would I what?" I prompt.

He clears his throat, but he doesn't make eye contact with me. The toe of his shoe kicks at the ground while he speaks to me,

"Would you want to spend some time together over the next couple of days before you leave?"

My stomach falls, but it isn't from dread, it's from excitement. It feels heavy yet light at the same time. I shouldn't feel this way, it isn't right, but once again, I'm answering before thinking, "Yes. Yes, I would like that. What do you have in mind?"

He shrugs, "I have some commitments that I can't get out of, but other than that maybe we can….I don't know… go to the fair that's in town? Get some meals together? See the guys? I'm sure they would love to see you, if you're game."

The thought of seeing those crazy men brings a smile to my face. It's been too long and while part of me is nervous to see them again, I know that it will be great too. "I would really like that. I'd like to spend some time with you. Like we used to." I tell him honestly, but then realize how that may sound. We aren't lovers anymore so I add nervously, "As friends."

He nods and smiles which makes my stomach start doing back flips. "Okay. I have to go to training now, but can I pick you up for dinner tonight?"

"Sure. I'd like that."

"Okay. I'll be at your hotel at six. Does that work for you?" I nod, and we both smile at each other awkwardly for a moment. "Are you leaving now? I'll walk you to your car."

"Yes, that would be great."

With one final look back at Hope, I follow Cole to my car and with a promise to see him later, drive off.

It was stupid to agree to this. I'm a nervous wreck and I've yanked every single item of clothing I brought with me out of my suitcase and discarded each one only to realize that left me with nothing.

Going out naked is certainly not an option. I considered going shopping to buy something, but quickly nixed that idea feeling as if it seemed too date like. And this is not a date; this is two people with a history taking some time to catch up. That's all.

Yanking on jeans and a yellow dolman top with a cute design, I slip my feet into some flats and then tackle my hair. Just as I'm finishing up, my phone rings. For a moment, I wonder if Cole had a change of heart and is calling me to cancel. One look at my phone changes that and I guiltily contemplate not answering his call again, but with a sigh I decide to stop avoiding a conversation.

"Hi, Blaine."

"Tatum, finally, hi. I've been trying to reach you. How are you?"

"I'm doing good. How are you?" He's tried calling several times today and I've ignored each one. I know he's checking in to see how I'm handling today – he knows what day it is. And I appreciate it, but I just haven't been able to talk to him about it. I'm not sure why.

"I'm missing you, and thinking about you. I know it's a tough day for you. So, how are you doing today - really?" There. There it is. The reason I haven't wanted to speak to him. It isn't the question, it's one that anyone would or could ask me if they knew why today is a tough day. It's his tone of voice. I've come to learn the difference between what I call his normal voice and his doctor voice. Right now, he's using his doctor voice on me. I guess this is what happens when you date someone that used to be your therapist. Perhaps it's something he simply can't shut off, but I wish he would. There have been many times when I've wanted him to be my boyfriend, my lover, my confidant, my friend, anything but my therapist. I want to be able to speak without feeling like everything I say is being evaluated.

"Tatum? Are you there?"

"Yes, sorry. My mind is wandering a bit, I apologize."

"It's understandable. It must be difficult – different for you this year– being there. Anything you need to talk about?"

I consider not telling him. Part of me doesn't really think it's his business and if I'm honest with myself that is definitely something I need to evaluate at another time. But, instead, I find myself blurting it out, maybe because it's at the forefront of my mind, "I saw Cole today."

"I wondered if maybe that would happen while you were there. How did it go?"

I'm not sure what I expected, or if I expected anything specific really. It's not like Blaine was going to act jealous, or tell me to get away from Cole, or beg me to come home. That's not like him, and I know that. Still, I find his response to be a let down. Again, something to think on I suppose. "It was…intense."

"And how would you define intense? What did it feel like? I recall that you two had a number of things that were left unstated. How do you feel having seen him?"

"I feel fine. I feel…lighter in some ways, but heavier in others."

"That's to be expected, Tatum. Would you like to elaborate?"

"Thank you, Blaine, but no." I mutter sarcastically.

"What was that?"

Lying, I say, "I said, I'm seeing him again."

"Well that's really good. Quite healthy, actually, assuming that seeing him involves civil conversation and not screaming and yelling. Although, some of that would be good too if indeed that is what you need. Just get out all of your feelings." He goes into complete therapist mode now. "In my opinion, I believe that seeing him will help you be able to fully let go in some ways and you'll finally be able to allow yourself to completely move forward. This is a big step toward your healing and it's not one that many people would be able to make. You should be proud of yourself for that. Give yourself a pat on the back."

He did not just say that. "Well, I'm glad you think so because we are having dinner tonight and will do things over the next couple of days until I leave."

"Sounds good. My advice would be to let yourself feel whatever it is that you need to. Whatever it is that will help you take positive steps forward. Expect that you will likely have a variety of emotions over the next couple days, and allow yourself to feel them."

"Okay. Thank you, doctor," I can't help but replay with exasperation. "Do be sure to send me a bill for this phone call."

I can hear his sigh and almost smile, feeling a little bit of glee that I managed to irk him like he's bothered me. He knows that this is a bone of contention between us, yet he can't turn it off. "Tatum, I just care about you, that's all."

"I know, Blaine. I know." There's a soft knock on the hotel door and the timing is perfect. "I've got to go. I'll talk to you later. Bye." I don't listen for a reply and press the end button on my phone. Standing from the bed, I nervously smooth the front of my shirt and then realize I'm being ridiculous. Moving quickly to the door, I open it and smile when I see Cole on the other side, also smiling.

"Ready?" he asks me and I nod in return.

"Yes. Let me just grab my purse." I gesture to the door and he holds it open while I dash to the bed and grab what I need. "So, where are we headed?" I ask while we walk to the elevators.

"You'll see."

"A surprise?"

"Yeah," he smiles, "a little bit of the past. A good part," he says with a smile and it warms me head to toe.

We're quiet on the drive to our destination; it feels awkward being together again. It's an odd combination of comfortable and uncomfortable; it's like your favorite flannel shirt that fit like a glove and was worn in all the perfect places all of the sudden gets shrunk in the dryer. It still feels familiar, but it's different now.

When we head east on the freeway, I immediately have a feeling that I know where he may be taking me. It isn't long before we pull into the exact place I was hoping we were going. I can't help but smile when it comes into view. I have so many memories of hanging out here and studying with Cole. They had great affordable food, but what we loved most was the atmosphere. It's almost as if they picked up a restaurant from the Midwest and plopped it into the middle of the Arizona desert. The property has big full trees in the front and in the back, with lush grass that has to be brought in from somewhere because it's certainly not Arizona's dry and itchy version. I can see that picnic tables are still scattered across the property, offering plenty of room to spread out. I'm hoping the inside hasn't changed.

"I love Porky Q's!" I smile and giggle a little at the name. "I'm happy that it's still here."

"Me too. I haven't been here in a long time. I thought it would be the perfect place to eat tonight."

Smiling, I practically bounce into the restaurant excited to eat some good food, and then feel embarrassed for my antics. Standing at the window where we place our order, Cole turns to me, "Do you want your usual? I'm sure they still have it."

"You remember what I liked?" He simply smiles and I nod eager to see if he's telling the truth. When he orders us both BBQ pork sandwiches and their homemade fries, making sure to get extra BBQ sauce on the side, I know he's not lying. I grab the number they use to track our order to our table, turn out the door, and head to find a place for us to sit. It isn't too crowded and I snatch us an inviting table in the corner.

Joining me on my side of the table, Cole and I spend more time looking around the large dining area than at each other. They have various award certificates, pictures and banners hanging up that weren't here before. There's pictures from some foodie TV show they appeared on and apparently won something on too. When our food is finally brought to our table, I can't wait to take my first bite and when I do, I'm not disappointed my sounds of delight making that apparent. They also make Cole laugh. "What?" I ask him innocently, mouth full, and unashamed that I'm not exactly worried about my manners.

"It's just your moans sound a bit x-rated."

I roll my eyes, "I'm not moaning."

"You're definitely moaning."

"Am not."

"Whatever you say."

"Remember when your mom catered in Porky Q's for your family birthday dinner that one year?" I ask changing the subject.

Cole smiles, and it's a genuine smile. It's big and full and he's holding nothing back. It makes my heart soar and heat burst in my stomach. "We thought she was sick or something."

I laugh at the memory, "That's because in her world, catering in food from somewhere else and not cooking is practically a sin."

"She laughed and said, 'No, I'm not sick, boy. I will be though if I don't figure out what in the hell they are putting on their BBQ sauce that makes it so damn good. Now take a bite and tell me what you think is in this stuff.'"

"Yes!" I nod. "And she kept muttering to herself and taking bites."

"I'm pretty sure she'd be unhappy if she knew how often we used to come here," he says.

"Did she ever figure it out?"

"The recipe?" He asks popping a fry into his mouth, and I nod. "Nope."

We both laugh and hell it feels good to be together like this. Our encounters so far have been emotionally charged, and laughing like this… well it surprises me how easy it comes. "Thanks for bringing me here."

He shrugs, "I'm glad we decided to do this, and to spend some time together before you leave."

"Me too." We stare at each other. I wish I could read his mind right now and know what he's thinking. His words from earlier today, 'not everything is what it seems' haunt me. There's no way I can just ignore that and not try to get to the bottom of what that means. "Cole..."

"Tell me more about art school," he interrupts. It makes me wonder if a look on my face tipped him off about my thoughts. He used to be good at reading me.

"What do you want to know?"

"I don't know... everything.... anything. I know we talked about it a little bit before, but I want to know more. What was your favorite thing about it? Are you happy you went? Is the school as good as what I read? Do you-"

"What you read?" I ask, my turn to interrupt. "What do you mean what you read?"

He looks down and I'm not sure he's going to answer. I watch him closely as he sighs, wipes his mouth with a napkin, and takes a drink of his soda. "I looked up information about the school, you know, back when you thought you wanted to go, before."

"Before? And you just happen to remember?"

"Again with asking me if I remember things. Like I told you before, I remember *everything*." His eyes stare into my own and for a split second I wonder if he's imagining me naked. I'm embarrassed that the thought even crosses my mind. Maybe it's the way he said 'everything' combined with the smirk on his face and the flash of heat I swear I saw for a second in his eyes. Pushing away my completely inappropriate thought, I take a sip of my drink as I find my mouth is suddenly dry.

Once I compose myself, I begin talking about school. "I loved it," I shrug. "I thought that given everything," I gesture between the two of us, "that I would have a hard time jumping into school again. Instead, doing just that worked really well...initially. I joined anything and everything I could. My schedule was loaded. I took extra painting classes, attended all kinds of lectures, basically anything I could. I even took a couple introduction courses for photography, and don't laugh, but I tried ceramics too."

"Why would I laugh?"

"Well, I guess you wouldn't about my taking the classes, but you'd definitely laugh at my work. I was awful at ceramics. I have a couple bowls and vases I made that are completely lopsided to prove it."

"It's okay, we can't all be good at everything."

I roll my eyes at his comment. "The problem was that while throwing myself into school worked for a little while and helped keep my mind busy, it also meant I wasn't dealing with anything that happened. It all came to a head when an instructor told us about a new project we were starting involving live models. They were quiet about the models. There was murmuring of course about if they would be nudes, animals, or whatever. So, when a mother with her beautiful baby showed up to our classroom to say it was not what I was expecting is an understatement. I mean, seriously? Of all things, that didn't even cross my mind."

I take another drink and for a moment think about how telling this story isn't difficult. Being with him feels easier, lighter. After having our blow up at the cemetery, I think maybe we got it out of our system. Said what we needed to say. I've come a long way, and that feels good, really good. Coming to Arizona was definitely the right thing to do. "When they sat down in the center of the room, surrounded by students eager to paint them, they just simply lived their life – in front of all of us. She held her baby, coddled her when she cried, changed her diaper, fed her, held her close – I couldn't look away. I kept imagining myself in her place with Hope in my arms. I couldn't move. At the end of class I hadn't painted a thing. My professor walked by my canvas at the end of class and questioned me. I completely broke down and became a sobbing mess."

"What did he do?"

"He was incredibly kind. He listened, and then gave me information for the college counselor so I could get a therapist recommendation. The good thing is that even though I was incredibly embarrassed, Professor Epstein held me accountable. He made sure I followed through with seeing the counselor."

"Was it the first baby you'd seen since Hope?"

"No, not at all. I mean, you can't go out anywhere without seeing a mother with her children, or a pregnant woman. For months I would notice them everywhere I went, as if they had shining beacons of light displaying them to my eyes. Even that was easier than having them in such a personal setting, sitting before me, silently asking me to put my artist hat on and make something beautiful from my pain."

"What did you do?"

"I went to the counselor after a couple reminders from my professor, then made an appointment with a therapist. I think I initially avoided it because of the hospital counselor I saw here. I felt like that person just went through the motions and didn't really help me at all. I wish I hadn't waited." I pause and take a drink before continuing. "The next day, class was still tough, but somehow I managed to begin painting. I pushed through the pain and my tentative brush strokes became more and more insistent. Soon I discovered that there was healing to be found in my art. Little by little I started to get better and better. Even though I rationally knew that losing Hope wasn't my fault, having a third party that was a professional help me understand the same thing, was life changing for me. I still struggle with it at times, but I'm better. Eventually, I didn't have to push through my pain anymore. It just became a part of me, a part of who I am, and not in a bad way. I learned that it's part of my story. And using that is how my pieces of Hope that you saw at the gallery came to be. I was finally able to allow myself to think of her in ways that weren't solely painful. To imagine how she would look, what she'd be doing. It was incredibly freeing."

"I have to admit I was a little worried when I saw all the paintings that maybe you had just shifted your grief to your art. That you used it as the only outlet."

I shrug, "I did at first, how could I not? Painting is an emotional outlet; it only makes sense my grief would be tied into it for a time. Not with those pieces though, they are nothing but love and light to me. Sure, there's a touch of sadness too, and regret, there always will be, but they are also so much more. I continued on with therapy for a while and it helped. It helped a lot."

"How did you end up having your own gallery show? It takes some artists years to get pieces into a gallery, let alone have their own showing."

"A cool requirement my school had for their painting courses was that a few times a year a local gallery in downtown Chicago partnered with our school. They would choose a theme, and we would all paint projects and submit them to the gallery. The themes were different each time - flowers, fruit, people, cities, sports, you name it. Our professors would take our finished pieces to the gallery owner and various paintings were chosen by him to be displayed. Each and every time, my painting was chosen."

"Wow, that's amazing. Although, I'm not really surprised."

"Not only were they chosen, they were sold every time too," I admit a little shyly.

"That's awesome, Tatum, but again, I'm not surprised. You've always been an extremely talented painter."

"Thank you, but I was shocked! From there I ended up finding out that the gallery owner was a friend of…a friend. My friend introduced us formally and my own showing progressed from there."

"Sounds like it's a friend you're lucky to have."

I hesitate, feeling uncomfortable talking about Blaine, although I'm not sure why. "Yes. Yes, lucky," I agree but say no more.

"Tell me about one of the pieces you painted. You said one was a sports theme. What did you choose?" He asks with a twinkle in his eyes knowing I'm not at all sports inclined. He may be sorry he asked.

"Well, actually, it was a piece of you."

The smile falls off of his face, "Of me?"

"Yes. I painted a fighter's profile, hands taped, head bowed in concentration and with sweat on his brow as he got ready for a fight."

"I would have loved to see it."

"I have a photo somewhere, I can send it to you."

"I'd like that."

"Even after everything…" I trail off not sure if I should continue. One look into his dark eyes and I forget why I was worried. "I may have been angry and hurt, but my time with you was one of the best times of my life. I always carried you with me, Cole. In here." I tap my heart and watch as his throat moves with a hard swallow. He nods and needing to move away from this subject, I ask him a question, "You said you are still fighting with the guys. How is that going?"

He takes a minute to shift gears, eyes still locked on mine. He blinks and looks down, shaking his head a little before returning his gaze to mine. "It's fine. I mean, fighting is fighting."

"You used to love it. Do you still?"

"There are parts of it I love. Parts of it I don't."

"Do you win?"

A smile curves his mouth, "Yeah, sometimes. I've learned a lot over the years, and I'm always learning from the guys too of course."

"I'm sure that's true. Does Coach Gillespie still train you?" I smile at the thought. I always loved that old man and he loved all the guys like sons.

"No. Not anymore."

"What? Why not? Is he okay?" Now that I think about it, he was getting up there in age before I left.

"He's great. Still working with Jax and the other guys sometimes. I've got a different coach now, and I train at a different gym."

"You don't train at Jax's gradfather's gym anymore? Why not?"

"I still go there as often as I can to work out and to see the guys, but my official training isn't done there any longer. And Jax actually owns the gym now. His grandfather passed away and left the gym to him."

"Wow. I remember Jax's dad being kind of an asshole. I bet that pissed him off."

Cole grimaces, "You have no idea."

"When is your next fight? Soon?"

"I have one coming up. I've been training pretty hard."

"Is it a big pay out?" I ask being nosey and smiling, just trying to make conversation and find out more about his life.

"It's not too shabby. Are you finished?"

Looking down at my empty food cartons I smile and nod. "Obviously." He laughs and takes my tray and his to the trashcan. "Ready?" he asks when he returns and I want to say no, but instead I nod. As we walk back to his car, all I can think about is how I'm not ready for the evening to end. I'm enjoying being in his company. Part of me battles with the feeling a bit, not wanting to turn it into anything that it isn't, but his eyes are full of something I'd like to be able to define – a sadness that's heavy and deep and it's as if he's just waiting for someone to care. Between that and his comment at the cemetery, I'm not ready to let go.

"You're quiet," he murmurs to me eyes on the road before us.

"Me? You're the quiet one."

He smiles, a flash of white against the darkness. "Yeah, but I'm always quiet."

"True."

"How about some ice cream? I was going to get some the other night, I had a craving, but didn't."

"Why not?"

"Because that happens to be the night I was handed a flyer that had your pretty face on it advertising your art show. Suddenly, seeing you seemed much more important."

"Wow, I rank higher than ice cream? How's that possible?" I tease, "It's so creamy and delicious."

He laughs softly and something about it makes goose bumps run up and down my arms. "If memory serves correctly, so are you Tatum, so are you."

"You did not just say that!" I laugh, but feel my insides heat at the same time. The car suddenly becomes stifling. His laugh rings out in the small space and I'm sure my cheeks are on fire. That's the thing about him. He can be quiet and then all the sudden will say something that takes you completely by surprise. That's always been his personality, and it's nice to know that he's being himself with me. And hearing his laugh again? It's the best sound I've heard in a long time.

"Sorry," he clears his throat, "but you kind of left yourself wide open to that one."

"It's okay, you're right I did. Too bad for you though."

"What do you mean?"

"Well too bad you'll never get to refresh your memory."

He laughs at my teasing, and when we arrive at the ice cream parlor, he wears a smile all the way inside. We smile as we eat our double scoops. Smile as he uses his thumb to remove ice cream from the corner of my mouth. Smile as he drops me off at my hotel. Smile after an all too brief hug and a promise to see each other tomorrow. And as I fall asleep that night, I find myself smiling into the night, hoping that Cole's smile follows me into my dreams.

CHAPTER NINE

Cole

I'm in an unbelievably good mood today. I was smiling like an idiot when I fell asleep and again when I woke up this morning. I can't turn the damn thing off. Usually my smile while working out is menacing; I usually picture my opponent's face instead of the bag I'm punching. It's a good motivator, but today? Today, I'm smiling a smile I haven't sported in five years. One I haven't felt like wearing since the day she left.

Even now as I pound the bag in front of me, my mind is elsewhere and I keep reliving the time I spent with Tatum last night. God, it felt so good to be with her again. It's different of course because we aren't together, but it's also the same in some ways too. I find myself falling back into old habits with her, like the sexual innuendo I made, and other times I feel like a stranger around her. It's a strange mixture that I'm trying to navigate my way through.

Problem is, I don't have long to navigate my way through anything with her. She leaves way too soon for that. My smile instantly falls, and I push the thought away electing not to go there right now. I can't, I'm not ready. I've known our time together is temporary, and I never expected to get more than a glance at her from the second I found out she was here. But having gotten more, it's like giving a drug addict his drug of choice after a long withdrawal. I want more and more, and because of this, the detox is going to be hell. It's going to be a blow to my heart once again.

"What the fuck, Cole?" Jerry slurs at my back making me swing around to stare at him. I didn't even hear him walk up to me. "Is there a reason you're staring at the bag instead of hitting it?"

"Uh, no." I mumble partly because I didn't realize I was staring and partly because I'm taken off guard by his appearance. He's been in the office since I arrived a few hours ago. I've been going through my routine, working hard and ignoring him. I know I have a fight in a couple days, so my lack of concentration certainly isn't helping, but hell, I work out every damn day. I've been training non-stop for five long years. I love it, but it's been wearing. I'm allowed an off day.

"I'm going to ask you this one more time. What the hell is going on with you? Your head has not been in the game this last week. Do I need to remind you that you have a fight in less than forty-eight hours? At this rate, you're going to get your ass kicked and you know what that means. No extra money going any-fucking-where."

"Shove it up your ass, Jerry. I'm tired of this shit. You and I both know that this little deal between us is about over, I don't care what you say. So go ahead and threaten me all you want, I don't care anymore."

"Oh, really? Is that right?" He laughs and I hate myself for the fact that my stomach sours at the sound. "So you don't care if I call up Jax and the other guys and tell them all about our little deal then? You know they've always been wondering why you put up with my shit." I'm shocked at his words because I've clearly underestimated the fact that he pays attention to what's going on and being said around him. I should have known better. I've slacked off and gotten too comfortable after five years I guess.

"Didn't think I knew about that did you? I know everything you little shit, remember that. Including the fact that you'd give anything for them not to know the reason I'm still hanging around even though Jax has tried his best to get rid of me." My stomach twists at the thought of them knowing what I've done. It's pathetic, but my pride can't take the blow. I've done everything I can to keep it from them over the years – they wouldn't understand. I've thought so many times about asking for help, to lay it all on the table, to take the beating to my dignity if it meant I could get out of this massive hell hole I willingly put myself in. But, I can't. The fact our deal is coming to an end makes me realize that it's likely they are going to find out anyway, but I can't let my mind go there. I don't want them to know that Jerry has had me by the balls all these years. They will never respect me again.

Jerry laughs again as if he can hear my internal thoughts, "Now, I don't know if you're in need of a fuck, or what. But get your ass out of here, take care of it, and then get back here the same time tomorrow to take care of business."

God, I hate him.

Without a word I walk away and instead of cleaning up in the locker room like I usually do, I grab my things and head home instead.

Hours later, I'm feeling better. Nothing a long shower, some food and a nap can't help. I'm about to head out to pick up Tatum for our date to the fair tonight when my phone rings. "Hello?"

"Cole, where the hell have you been? I haven't seen you in like… two…three…days?"

"Zane, hey." Zane has been one of my friends for years; we met in high school. Zane and Jax have been friends since they were kids, but other than Tyson, I met the Zane, Jax, Levi, Dylan, and Ryder in high school. We all became fast friends because we were on the high school wrestling team together and managed to take number one in the state two years in a row. We all received small scholarships to Arizona State University and then went on to fight in the MMA too. Tyson we met when he started working out at Jax's gym and got into MMA later. If guys have best friends, they would all be mine. They're my brothers, which is why it's been so hard to lie to them for five years. "I've been working hard with the fight coming up. Sorry I haven't been by the gym."

"Yeah, Ryder was going on and on about not seeing you lately, I told him I'd give you a call. When are you going to come by?"

"Is that Cole?" I hear Dylan ask in the background. "Tell him to get his ass here before Ryder starts crying like a little girl."

"I live right down the hall from him, all he has to do is come knock on my door."

"Yeah, that's what we said, and according to him he's tried and you haven't been home the last couple times he's knocked. So, we are checking in to make sure all is well. That Jerry hasn't killed you and disposed of your body or something."

"Ha. Ha."

"Glad you're not dead and rotting somewhere!" I hear Tyson say into the phone.

"Get the hell away from the phone, man, I'm trying to talk to him," Zane says in annoyance. And then I hear a bunch of shuffling and murmuring that I can't make out.

"Fuck! That hurt asshole!" Zane says and I can hear Tyson laughing in the background.

"Well, thanks for caring, but I'm fine." No response, just more shuffling and name-calling. "Zane! Zane!" I yell trying to get his attention back.

"Zane can't come to the phone right now," Levi says into the phone.

"Where's Jax?" I ask. "You guys clearly need a babysitter."

"Do not," Levi says.

"Give me that!" Zane says. "Sorry, man. These guys are adolescents."

"Yeah, I know." Hell if I don't have a smile on my face from this call. Idiots. "Thanks for calling, but I'm good."

"You going to come by soon?"

"Yeah, I'll be there tomorrow, which reminds me, uh… I need to ask you for a favor. I'll have someone with me when I come in tomorrow…"

"Dude, if it's Jerry, you know Jax isn't going to let that fly."

"It's not Jerry, I know better than that. It's…Tatum."

"Wait, did you say Tatum? *The* Tatum? The Tatum you dated back in college? Tatum that left and you were never…?" I can hear the hesitation in his voice.

"Never, what?"

"Come on, man. You know you were never the same after she left."

Running my hand through my hair at his words, I sigh, "Yes, it's that Tatum."

"Fuck man. She's back? You okay?"

"When did we become women that share our feelings and shit?"

"Screw you. It's not my fault you don't talk about shit. Now answer the damn question."

I'm grateful for the fact I have friends that care even though I can't help yanking his chain about it. "No, she's not back. She's just here for a visit and we ran into each other. Sort of. It's kind of complicated."

"Isn't it always?" he sighs.

"She wants to come to the gym tomorrow to see all of you if you're going to be around."

"You know we will be. We always are for the most part."

"Yeah, I know, can you give the guys a heads up? I just want to avoid any awkward comments and surprises I guess, I don't know."

"I'll handle it."

"Thanks."

"Yeah, no problem. And, Cole, next time don't stay away without touching base with Ryder, alright? He becomes downright moody when he hasn't seen you in a while. You guys have a complicated bromance."

"We don't have a bromance."

"Whatever, man," he laughs. "Deny it all you want, we know the truth."

"Look, I can't help it if he can't go a few days without seeing me. I have that affect on people."

"See you tomorrow," he laughs as he hangs up, but not before I hear him yell Ryder's name, no doubt eager to tell him about our conversation.

Anxious now to get out the door, I arrive at the fair in record time. Tatum asked to meet here because she had some things to wrap up at the gallery this afternoon and wasn't sure how long she'd be and thought it would be easier to come straight here. It's a nice night, and I'm glad I had the idea to come here. It's lighthearted entertainment and should be fun.

Hesitant for a moment to get out of the car, I find myself reveling in my nerves. It's a good feeling, one that's been foreign for far too long. It isn't that I haven't been with a woman since she left, that's not true at all. I've had far too many bumbling, meaningless, ridiculous, encounters. Some embarrassing, some I can barely remember, and others I would do anything to forget. They've all had one purpose – taking care of a need and in the process relieving my loneliness – at least for a few moments. Hell, I've been lonely. I guess that's the ramifications of accepting a deal like I did, one you can't tell anyone about without consequence. Quick and no strings was the smartest choice; the least risky. Keeping distance from everyone for the last five years emotionally was the smartest thing to do. Not because I'm trying to protect myself, but because I'm taking care of her. Always her.

Closing my eyes for a minute, I try to hold onto my nervous feeling a little longer, revel in it. The excitement of seeing her face, wondering if I will risk trying to brush my skin against hers, just a finger against her hand or a brush of my thumb across her cheek. I want to touch her. I want to see her smile, hear her laugh, watch her hair blow in the breeze and see happiness shine in her eyes. Just one more time, once more before she leaves.

Letting go of my thoughts for now, I get out of my car, roll my shoulders back a few times then start heading toward the fair entrance where we agreed to meet. It's crowded and I maneuver through a lot of people, my eyes roaming the crowd. I spot her right away. She's standing near the ticket booth. She's wearing jeans that are molded to her body and a bright red shirt. Her hair is pulled back a little from her face and her lips are painted a bright red that matches her shirt. As I walk toward her, she doesn't see me, so I'm free to stare at her lips. I imagine what it would be like to walk up to her, take her in my arms and kiss her senseless. Like I used to. I wonder what it would be like to hold her in my arms again, and call her mine.

The crowd parts and she sees me. A smile instantly lights up her face and it causes a slight hitch in my step. How many times have I thought about her smile over the years? I thought I'd only ever see it again in my dreams. It's better than I remember.

"Hi," she says, eyes full of excitement.

"Hi, you look amazing," I tell her honestly.

She looks down shyly, "Thank you. I went ahead and got us both tickets to get in."

I frown, "This was my treat."

"How about you buy me an elephant ear instead?"

"Deal," I nod. We hand our tickets over to get inside and then stand still after taking a few steps past the entrance and look around. "What do you want to do first?" I ask.

"Eat! I'm starving," she admits.

"Food it is then." Without thinking about it, I grab her hand and begin moving in and out of the crowd toward the tents and trailers where the food is located. Her hand tightens in my own and I enjoy the weight of it. When we reach the vendors, we take a minute to look around. There's everything from pizza and hot dogs to deep friend twinkies and the elephant ear I'll be buying at some point. "What are you in the mood for?"

"Hmm…" she taps her finger on her chin as she looks around and decides. She's never been shy about eating and it's something I've always loved about her. "Everything looks good to me. What are you hungry for?"

"I'm thinking-"

"You ask." I hear loudly behind me.

"No, you do it."

"Fine. Um, excuse me," a voice says even louder behind me. I turn around to find two boys that can't be anymore than twelve or so staring at me. They each take a step backwards when I face them, making me stifle a smile. The brave one and clearly the designated speaker asks, "Are you Cole 'Rampage' Russell?" I can't help but smile and nod. "I told you it was him," the boy says to his friend.

"And you are?" I ask.

"My name is Brandon and this is Joe," he jabs a finger at his friend. "We're big fans. We've seen you on TV."

"Well thank you for watching."

"Can we have your autograph?"

"Oh, um, sure…" I say looking around for something to write on. I grab a couple napkins from a nearby food stand and wait to ask a worker for a pen when Tatum interrupts. "Here you go."

I look up and find her holding out a pen with a smile on her face. "Thank you," I nod and smile. Quickly scribbling out a note to both boys I sign it and hand it to them.

"Wow, thank you so much. I can't wait to tell my dad I met you!"

"You're welcome."

"I want to be a fighter just like you some day!" The little boy Brandon tells me.

"Oh yeah? Want some advice?"

"Sure," he says and leans forward anxious to hear what I'm going to tell him.

"First, and most importantly, stay in school. Compete on your wrestling or MMA team if your school has one, but stay in school.

That's really important. Stay in school all the way through college okay?" They each nod solemnly. "And the second thing is to never ever give up. Taking a bit of a beating when you first start is normal, it's all part of learning how to fight. If you stick with it you'll end up becoming more like a hammer, the one that gives the beating, instead of the nail, the one that takes it. Understand?" Once again they nod. "Alright, it was nice to meet you. Thanks for saying hi to me."

"Bye Mr. Rampage," Joe says and I suppress a laugh and give them a wave.

Turning back to Tatum to give her the pen she loaned me, I find her smiling, but there's a little sadness on her face too. "Cole, you'll make a really great dad one day. I always knew you would."

I can't help it, I take her into my arms and I kiss the top of her head. Sometimes there are moments when words aren't necessary, a touch, gesture, smile, look, it says more than words could and this is one of those moments. Pulling away from her, I smile and wait for her to return it. "Come on, let's eat, I'm starving. I'm thinking a good 'ol fashioned hot dog, what do you say?"

She smiles, and the melancholy washes away, "Sounds perfect."

With hotdogs in our hands moments later, we walk around and decide to sit around where a band is performing. Quiet at first, she finally turns to me when she's finished eating, "Does that happen often?"

"What's that? The boys?"

"Yeah, that was adorable."

"From time to time," I shrug. After taking the last bite of my hot dog, I wipe my mouth and then raise my brows at her, "I have an important question."

"What's that?"

"What should I win for you?"

She laughs, "What do you mean?"

"Well this is a fair isn't it? That means games!" With a laugh, I grab her hand again and we head toward various games. The first game we step up to is where you throw darts at balloons and the more you pop the bigger the prize. With my five darts, I only manage to pop three. Tatum laughs and cheers me on the whole time, which makes me smile non-stop. When they hand me a rainbow colored unicorn I look at it awkwardly, but Tatum jumps up and down and claps. When she takes it from me, she gives me a kiss on my cheek.

"Yay! I love it!" As she pulls away from me her cheek brushes against mine slow and soft. Our eyes connect and I want to kiss her right then. Instead, I vow to play every damn game they have there to win her things if that's going to be my reward. We laugh the whole time. I play a basketball game trying to make as many baskets as I can in sixty seconds, I try to knock down a bunch of bottles with softballs, shoot ducks in a pond and even lose horribly trying to win her a goldfish that would probably die before we even left the park. I've won her several little items and happily received a kiss each and every time. I'm sure it's not my imagination when this time it seems the kiss lasts a little longer. I'm thinking that I haven't had this much fun in a long time when we walk up to a game that I know I can't lose.

Tatum laughs, "What the hell? This isn't your typical fair game."

"It's like they knew I would be here."

She rolls her eyes, "Alright hotshot, let's see what you've got."

"Step right up, sir, see if you can win a prize for the lady."

"I can definitely win a prize for my lady, but I want to make a deal," I tell him.

He crosses his arms and eyes me, "What kind of deal?"

"I bet you I can reach the highest score, on the first try, and if I do, I want to trade in all of this," I gesture to the grouping of animals I've won for her, "for that," I point at the giant blue monkey hanging from the top of the tent.

"The high score on the first try?" He smirks like I'm an idiot.

"Yep," I tell him.

"Deal. In fact, if you get the high score on the first try you don't even have to give me any of the other animals she has as a trade in, she can have it all."

Looking at Tatum, I smile and almost laugh. She's already holding a yellow elephant, an orange dog, a big yellow smiley face, and a purple and white long worm thing or it might be a snake, I can't tell. "What do you think, Tay?" I ask, my old nickname for her coming out without thought.

"Let's see what you've got hotshot."

The game is simple, it's a punching bag hanging from a machine. You punch the bag as hard as you can and the machine gives you a score based on your punch. The highest score is 999. Walking up to the bag, just before I reach it I throw a few practice punches. "Whooo," Tatum cheers and it makes me laugh. "Looking good!"

"Alright," I say out loud. "Here goes." And then I punch the bag as hard as I can. Tatum walks up next to me immediately and when the numbers move up to 999 so fast it's a blur, she starts jumping up and down like a kid and cheering.

"Wow, good job man," the fair worker tells me while grabbing and stepping up on a chair to get the huge monkey down for Tatum. A few people cheer around us and I smile and nod not even realizing I had an audience. When he hands Tatum the monkey, I laugh and pull my phone out to take a picture. It's almost as big as she is.

She poses with the monkey, it's arm around her shoulders, and another kissing it's cheek. "I'm going to name him Rampage, after you."

Taking some of the other animals from her, I laugh. "How about we ride the Ferris wheel before we get you that elephant ear?"

"Sounds perfect."

The guy working the wheel tells us we can leave all her winnings with him while we ride, so we do. Side to side in the cart, I put my arm around Tatum and give her a squeeze. "I'm glad we did this."

"Me too. I'm having so much fun. Thank you for this."

We smile at each other and in that moment, the cart hits the top of the wheel and the moon is the perfect backdrop to Tatum. The light from the moon makes her hair shine and a few strands of hair press against her flushed cheek as they blow in the breeze. She's never looked more beautiful and I ache inside, fucking ache. As we continue to swing around in a circle, I want to say so many things. Tell her how I've thought about her every single day. I want to tell her that while losing her is something I'll never get over, I'd do it the same way all over again if it meant seeing her like this, right now. Because I've convinced myself that my sacrifice has been worth it. That she wouldn't have been able to be like this again without it. That the decision I made for both of us was the right one. The thing is, I'm not sure that I could bare it to think differently, so I'll just live in this reality then instead.

Reaching out, I can't help it, I brush a thumb across her cheek. "Tatum…" I whisper, and she moves toward me, and I her. My eyes are solely on her mouth and I can imagine just what they would feel like pressed against mine.

When the ride stops suddenly it takes me a minute to realize that the ride is over. The ride monitor holds the foot rest toward the ground waiting. It's our turn to get off. Clearing my throat, I regret that the moment is broken, but know it's the right thing.

"Come on." We grab her plush animals and head to get her an elephant ear. She wants just the plain one with powdered sugar. We take a seat and people watch while we eat, laughing at the conversations around us.

When she looks at me, she's got powdered sugar in the corner of her mouth. Smiling, I point, "You've got a little…"

"What?"

"Sugar, in the corner of your mouth."

She swipes at it, but it doesn't come off. I use my thumb to brush it away, and she whispers, "Thank you." When I look at her, her eyes are staring at my mouth. I don't think twice. The look in her eyes is all I need. I tilt her chin up, then press my mouth to hers. It's hesitant at first, lips that used to know each other so well, rediscovering each other again. When she sighs and parts her lips just so, I groan and kiss her like I've been wanting to all night. I nibble on her bottom lip, I slide my tongue against hers, I cup the side of her face, tangle my hand in her hair. I try to make up for the five years I haven't been able to kiss these lips in one moment.

When we pull away, we're both breathing hard. Panting we stare into each other's eyes. "Your car," she says, her voice raspy.

"My car?"

"Yes. Let's go to your car," she says breathlessly and finally what she's saying clicks. Without a word I get up, grab the huge monkey in one arm and her hand in the other and lead the way to my car, completely abandoning our food. I'm a man on a fucking mission, I dodge and move around the crowd quickly and when we get to my car, I throw her prizes in the trunk and open the passenger door for her.

Once inside, I move my seat back and stare at her. We stare at each other. I'm not sure who moves first, maybe it was the same time. All I know is that we collide. Her hand is on my face, her lips on mine. My hand is in her hair again, my moth moving against hers, my tongue darting in and out of her mouth, tasting her, relishing her. She tastes of strawberries and sugar and I don't think I'll ever have enough.

I'm shocked when she pushes my shoulders back and next thing I know she's crawling over the console and straddling my lap. When her center presses against mine, we groan. Her hips jut and push, grinding against me, seeking friction. Her lips find mine again and my hand is at the small of her back, and then under her shirt slowly sliding up her side.

There's an annoying sound in the back of my mind and on some level I realize it's a phone ringing. We both ignore it and eventually it stops. Her hips move against me again and I'm lost. All I care about is her body against mine, the softness of her skin, and the path my hand is headed. I move to the front of her chest and moan when I feel the lace of her bra. "Tatum," I whisper and the sound is full of want and need.

"Yes," she says, her own hand under my shirt and on my bare skin, squeezing and scratching. She rips my shirt up my stomach, her nails scrape over my abs and play at the button of my jeans. Holy fuck, I think as I adjust my hips and it makes her head fall back on her shoulders, so I kiss her neck, tease her ear. I push her shirt up and bare one of her breasts to me. Just as I lean forward to take the hard peak into my mouth, there's that noise again. Insistent. Loud.

Tatum pulls away from me so quickly, the absence of her body heat feels shocking. Her big blue green eyes stare into mine and before I can ask her what's wrong, she slides out of my lap and reaches toward her phone. Taking it from her purse, she looks at the screen and presses the button shutting it off.

She tucks her hair behind her ear, takes a deep breath and straightens her clothes. The mood is clearly broken if the look on her face is any indication and I can't quite decide how I feel. "I'm sorry," she whispers not facing me.

Taking a deep breath, I take in the fogged windows and my skewed clothes and tighten my hands into fists. It's the only way I can keep myself from reaching out and touching her and I'm sure it's not what she would like from me at the moment.

Pulling down my shirt, I breathe in and out wishing the blood would leave my cock, so I can think clearly once more. She turns in her seat and opens her mouth like she wants to say something and shuts it again. I decide to save her the trouble, "So," I begin. "Who's the guy?"

Her eyes, big and round snap to mine, "Cole?" she says my name in question, but I'm not sure what she's asking. How I know? What I mean?

"I saw you with him." Her brow furrows in confusion. "The night I was given the flyer and saw information about your show, I went to the gallery right away. I looked in the window and after a few minutes, you appeared. Not long after that, a man walked up to you and it was obvious that you're together."

"You knew I was with someone and you kissed me anyway?"

"Whoa, how is this my fault?"

She lets out a breath, and shakes her head. "It's not." She's quiet for a minute, "He was my therapist."

"Come again?"

"My boyfriend. He was my therapist in Chicago. The man I saw to help me deal with everything."

I can barely get out my words, "You're boning your therapist? Isn't that a conflict of interest?"

"Cole!"

"What? Tell me right now he didn't take advantage of you," I demand feeling a tightening in my chest at the thought.

"No. He didn't take advantage of me. It just…happened."

"Do you love him?"

"What?" She asks wide-eyed and I remain quiet because I know she heard me. She sighs heavily and the fact that she isn't answering me immediately makes my stomach sour a little, and yet, in the back of my mind something is telling me she doesn't. Because I know her, and if she was completely in love with this guy, she wouldn't be kissing and grinding against me. "Honestly, I thought I was before. And I don't mean before seeing you this week, I mean if you had asked me six months ago, I would have said yes. But, I'm not. I know I'm not. I've been struggling with my feelings for a while, and I'm sorry."

"Sorry? For what?"

"I'm sorry that I kissed you and…" she gestures between us and her eyes drop to my lap and look away. I almost want to laugh, I'm sure I'm smirking at the very least. "It's not right. I'm feeling confused. Confused about Blaine…and you…"

"I'm not complaining."

She smiles, "No, I guess you aren't." She bites her lip and looks at the window for a second. She laughs a little at the foggy windows and makes a heart with her finger. "I should go."

"You don't have to go. It's okay. I'll keep my hands to myself."

"Well actually, now that you say that, if you knew that I had a boyfriend, why didn't you say something before?"

I could tell her that it's because I don't give a fuck who she's with, that if she wanted to kiss me any time, any where, I would kiss her back. I could tell her that I was so caught up in the moment and in being with her, that her having a boyfriend didn't even occur to me. I could tell her that I've dreamed about having one more chance to kiss her again and I wasn't about to turn down an opportunity. But I don't say any of that. I say something much more. I tell her the complete truth. "Tay, you're the love of my life. We could be apart five more years; ten, twenty, it doesn't matter. I will always remember kissing you and how it makes me feel. Right or wrong, good or bad, boyfriend or no boyfriend, everything else will always fall away when I'm with you. I'm lost in you."

I know I've taken her off guard; it's evident in the downward turn or her mouth, the shininess of her eyes, the tenseness in her shoulders. "God, Cole. I don't know what to say."

"Say, you'll still see me tomorrow." I change the subject giving her room to breathe.

"Yeah," she nods her head. "Still want me to meet you at your place?" Her voice trembles a little and I'm not sure if it's because of my confession or at the thought of being alone with me in my apartment.

"Yes, please do. As soon as you get there, we'll walk over to the gym, okay?"

"Okay. Good night, Cole. I had a really great time."

"So did I."

We get her winnings from the trunk, and she leaves. I make sure she gets to her car okay and remain still when she takes off. Hands trembling, mind turning, heart aching, I start my own car, and head home.

CHAPTER TEN

Tatum

My mind has been spinning all day long. Cole and I don't have plans to meet until early evening because he had to train today so I slept in, did some shopping at the mall and enjoyed a nice lunch. I topped it off by treating myself to a massage at the hotel. It felt so nice, and something I haven't done in a long time, yet, I had trouble fully being in the minute. Rather, the entire time my thoughts were consumed with the night before and I am in total ambivalence. Even my masseuse told me my shoulders were in knots and helped to rub out some tension.

I had a really nice time with Cole last night. Maybe too nice of a time, I don't know. What I do know, is that it was the old us. The old Cole and Tatum, and it felt amazing. We had fun together, laughed, teased each other, and simply enjoyed being together. Like we used to. When we were together, we rarely had a dull moment. Even when I was nose deep in a book and he was watching TV or studying, simply being next to each other was enough. Thinking about leaving the day after tomorrow makes me feel sick to my stomach. I'm not ready to go. Part of me wonders if I ever will be.

What am I thinking? This is absolutely ridiculous. I came here for my art exhibit – nothing more, nothing less. Seeing Cole was unexpected, a surprise, a good one at that, but I have a life. And he is not a part of it. That's old news. We are different people. Five years change people. I cannot afford to project more on to this than it really is. So, while it's been nice to obtain closure, which is something I needed even if I didn't realize it, I still have a lot of questions and confusions. However, keeping my distance and continuing along the trajectory that I have been pursuing is imperative. Thinking otherwise will just end in disaster and who needs that? But what am I to make of the fact that many of my prior questions and concerns have managed to fall away the last couple of days. Truth is, I've been able to live in the moment in a comfortable manner that is not typical – at least it hasn't been in a really long time.

And then there's Blaine. He tried calling me again last night and I didn't answer - I couldn't. I'm not sure what I want to say to him yet. The thing is, I should feel guilty for letting myself go that far with Cole but I don't, not at all. God, in that moment all I could think about was taking my clothes off – taking his clothes off. I wanted to touch him, feel him against me, explore his body, see what's familiar and what's new. Thoughts of Blaine didn't even enter my mind the entire night. That in its self is very telling about where my mind and most importantly my heart is where he's concerned. As if that wasn't enough, when I was shopping today I found myself looking at lingerie, imagining myself wearing it for Cole. I walked away, but then went back and bought it. In fact, I bought everything that caught my eye that I loved. Hell, I'm wearing some of it now. I need clarity and feel a bit out of control, and confused. What the hell am I doing?

I'll always love Blaine for helping me through the hardest thing I've ever been through. He was exactly who I needed at that specific time in my life, but that time has passed. Do I love him? No, not romantically. The idea of spending the rest of my life with him, or even this next chapter, is not appealing. So what am I doing? Has he become my emotional or therapeutic security net? If that were true, why does his therapeutic style annoy me? And why did I have to come here to realize this, to be honest with myself about this? Perhaps I've not been provided enough distance or time to think this through. I wish I had a friend I could confide in; one that would help stimulate this level of honesty with myself, but I don't. I do appreciate Blaine, and all he has done for me, but we are not aligned on what we want from this relationship. Of that I am sure. How exactly I'll communicate that to him, I don't know, but it needs to happen. I owe him that much.

Pushing my jumbled thoughts away when I pull into the parking lot at Cole's apartment building, I shut off my car and take a few calming breaths. Taking another look at myself in the mirror, I catch the look of excitement in my eyes at seeing him again. Closing them tightly, I try to calm myself as well as the desire I have to analyze it. I don't want to think too hard about my feelings right now. I do know that I feel like I'm on the precipice of something, but I don't know what. I feel both excitement and foreboding at the thought. I know without a doubt my life will be changed when I leave Arizona again. How could it not?

It doesn't take me long to find his apartment, and I've barely knocked before the door swings open. "Hey," Cole says smiling at me. I take in his simple black t-shirt and jeans and smile. It's comforting that some things never change.

"Hi," I reply with a smile of my own, feeling both hope and uncertainty about him inviting me inside. He turns around and grabs his keys and I use the opportunity to take a quick look around. His place looks pretty simple. Tidy, no decorations, sparse furniture – a lot of black from what I can tell. There are entryways to two other rooms, but I don't know what they are because the doors are closed. I'm assuming a bedroom and bathroom. Before I can look around more, he steps out and closes and locks the door behind him.

He gestures for me to walk in front of him out of the complex and down the stairs, "How was your day?" he asks.

"It was good. I slept in and decided to go shopping. I hit some of my old favorite boutique stores; they don't have any of them back home."

"Was one of them that little soap shop that you used to love?"

"Yes! How did you know?" He shrugs and I laugh. "I was delighted to find that it's still open. I was in there forever and then finally bought a few things; choosing wasn't any easier than now, than it used to be before."

"I know you used to love it. Your favorite was their bath ball things."

"Bath bombs," I say with a laugh. "And I still love them. I stocked up. And I got a massage at the spa today too."

"Sounds fancy."

As soon as we walk inside the gym, nostalgia hits me. It's a combination of seeing that the place looks the same - the octagon in the center, all the weights, and punching bags – and what is probably testosterone in the air. We've barely made it a few steps inside when Zane is in front of us. His hair is in a Mohawk and his muscles and tattoos are on full display in his sleeveless tank and shorts. "Tatum, hi gorgeous," he smiles and I find myself immediately returning it. "It's been too long."

"Zane, hi. It's really good to see you."

"And you." He turns to Cole and his demeanor instantly changes from flirtatious to annoyed, "About time you showed up motherfucker. We've been waiting for you all damn day."

"Well that's your problem. I didn't know for sure when we would be by, which is why I didn't give you a time." He rolls his eyes at Zane and mumbles to me, "And if a few of them happened to leave before we got here, then fine."

Laughing, I turn to Zane, "Well I'm glad they waited. I want to see everyone." Cole sighs, Zane smiles and holds his arm out to me. I take it and he escorts me to the octagon. A couple guys are sparring inside and others are egging them on. When we approach, Zane whistles loudly capturing everyone's attention immediately. "Look who decided to finally grace us with his presence," Zane says jerking his thumb at Cole.

"Would you knock that shit off? You act like I haven't been here forever. I didn't realize you have that much difficulty functioning without me," Cole replies in exasperation.

"Whoa," a voice says loudly drowning out the rest. I turn and see Levi standing there staring at me with a perplexed look on his face. I smile, but before I can say hello he looks at the guys and then points a finger at me, "You guys see her too, right?"

"See who?" Jax asks looking at him in amusement as he walks past him and hugs me. Jax is bigger than the rest of the guys, but as kind as they come. He hugs me tightly and pulls back looking into my eyes, flashing me dimples that would make any woman swoon. "It's really good to see you, Tatum."

"Thank you," I tell him honestly. "It's good to see you too. It's been a long time."

"Too long," he says and steps back but not before squeezing my upper arm tenderly. The guys were really great when Cole and I lost Hope. I remember them sitting shifts at our apartment, just eager to be around and help in any way possible whether it was bringing us food or taking out the trash. I couldn't leave my bedroom for a full week without tripping over one of them around somewhere, always kind, always asking what I needed and how they could help. I never thanked them for that, or fully appreciated it at the time.

"So you guys do see her then. Tatum. That's Tatum," Levi says slowly.

"Sorry, man," Zane says to Cole, "I told everyone that she was coming in except Levi. He wasn't around when I gave them a heads up."

"Hi, Levi," I say taking in his blonde hair and bright green eyes. He's still got the whole surfer boy look going on like he did years ago, only now his face is more mature, his body more muscular.

He runs up to me and gives me a hug practically bowling me over in his haste, "What the hell, Levi?" Cole asks, "Back the hell up before you hurt her," he demands protectively. Levi remains with his arms wrapped around me.

"Really, Levi. I had no idea I meant this much to you," I laugh and manage to pull myself out of his arms.

"I can't help it. It's kind of like the band is back together."

"Oh good god," Ryder says as he walks toward me. He scowls at Cole, and then takes me into his arms. "Hi, doll. It's good to see you."

"You too," I tell him and allow myself to be cocooned in his arms for a minute before I step back and look into his bright blue eyes and smile. When he smiles back, I find a deep happiness there that I don't remember from years ago. He's always practically secreted sensuality from his pores, but if you looked deep enough you could see pain that he tried very hard to hide and it came out in vulnerable moments. I'm surprised and happy to find that it's not there any longer. I'd be dead if I didn't think he was sexy, they all are. It's a damn bonanza of sexy up in here, it's ridiculous, but I feel contentment from him and it must be contagious because I find myself feeling calm.

"Tatey-girl, long time no see," Dylan smiles as he takes his turn hugging me next.

"I still hate that nickname, Dillie-poo."

He laughs, "Well, tell me that I'm at least still your favorite ginger."

"Always," I laugh.

Lastly, I see another guy that I don't recognize. He didn't go to college with us and I never saw Cole with him when I was here. "Tatum, this is Tyson. Tyson, this is Tatum. She and I dated five years ago and she went to college with all of us. That's why she knows everyone."

"Tatum, hi, it's nice to meet you," Tyson says quietly but with a lazy grin as he shakes my hand. Yeah, he fits right in with these guys, that's for sure. He's shirtless and I'm trying not to stare at all the skin before me. Because there's a hell of a lot of skin around me.

"Nice to meet you too," I tell him returning his handshake.

"I hope you two don't mind, but when we heard you were coming we made arrangements to go grab some dinner over at The Speckled Gecko," Jax says referring to the Mexican food place only a block away. "You game?" Jax asks us and I look at Cole at the same time he looks at me. I smile and nod to let him know without words that I'm fine with the plan. "Okay, sure," he says and amid cheers and comments about how hungry they are, the guys disperse to get whatever they need – hopefully and also regrettably, that includes some shirts.

"Let's go on ahead of them." Cole says and I nod and follow him out the door. It's a nice night out and I inhale deeply when we step outside.

"I can smell an orange blossom close by. I love that smell. Not long after I moved, I felt really home sick. I went to a beauty store that carried hundreds of perfumes and smelled samples of anything claiming to have orange as the primary base. I just wanted to have something that reminded me of home."

"Did you find one?"

"No, I never did." Cole's eyes are sad when he looks at me, which was not my intent. "I'm excited," I tell him and smile and feel delight when his mouth curves up in response.

"For?"

"To eat! I haven't eaten at a Mexican place since I've been back yet, so this is perfect. I'm thinking a margarita is in order too."

The place isn't too busy which is surprising given it's dinner time and as soon as Cole walks in the hostess smiles, "Hi, Cole," she says and I swear she sounds breathless. "Long time no see." She's smiling suggestively at him and I frown. I don't like it, and really would prefer not to have a side of slut with my dinner. It isn't like I have any claim to Cole, but good god I want to smack that look off her face. Or scratch it off with my nails. Either would suit me just fine.

"Hi Fannie," he says and I snort. Out loud. Because that is not at all the name I was expecting to hear. I can see Cole look at me out of the corner of my eye, but I don't react. Fannie on the other hand scowls at me, so I give her a knock out smile.

"Jax called earlier, so we have tables ready for you," she says now completely ignoring me and smiling even more widely at Cole.

"Great," he says and placing a hand at the small of my back indicates I should go before him. His touch makes tingles travel up my spine and I shiver. If he notices, he doesn't say a word. When we arrive at the table, he pulls the chair out for me and after I sit, he takes the seat next to mine.

"What was that all about?" Cole asks with a raised brow.

"What?" I ask in what I hope is an innocent manner.

"The fact that you looked like you wanted to cut Fannie up into little pieces."

"I don't know what you're talking about," I shrug and immediately order a margarita when the waitress arrives at our table happy to divert his train of thought.

The guys start to arrive one at a time. When Jax arrives, my mouth falls open at the sight. He's holding a little girl, no more than one year old in his arm, and is holding hands with a beautiful woman at his side. It's clear they are very much in love and they make a sweet family unit.

"I had no idea Jax is a dad," I tell Cole in surprise. Before he can respond Jax is at the table and introduces us immediately. "Tatum, I'd like you to meet Rowan, my lady," he says making Rowan laugh. "Rowan, this is Tatum, an old…friend of Cole's."

"Hi, Tatum. It's very nice to meet you." She smiles at Cole and gives him a one armed hug.

"It's nice to meet you too. And who is this beautiful girl in your arms, Jax?"

His smile could light up a room, "This little pumpkin is Rowan's daughter, Lily." After he introduces us, his smile falls a little and he looks at me as if he's apologizing for the fact they have a little girl with them. I smile at him encouragingly and get up out of my seat. Walking toward them, I take her sweet little hand in mine, "Hi, Lily. You're a gorgeous little thing."

Rowan and Jax smile and Lily smiles at me as if she knows I've just complimented her. When they turn to get her buckled into a high chair, I return to my seat and smile at Cole. "Jax and Rowan met when Rowan was in labor with Lily." My eyes widen at this news and he nods and laughs, "I'll have to tell you the story later."

"I look forward to that," I tell him.

Once Lily is settled Jax and Rowan take a seat and Rowan immediately picks up the menu making Jax laugh. "I don't know why you're looking at it babe, you always get the same thing."

"Yeah, but what if I change my mind? Today, could be the day."

"We'll see," he smiles an indulgent smile at her and I'm mesmerized by the two of them until I'm distracted by Tyson's arrival. He's got a gorgeous blonde on his arm, and he tells me her name is Sydney. She immediately sits next to Rowan and the two of them start chatting with Jax and Tyson looking on with a smile.

"Tyson is Rowan's brother," Cole explains quietly. "The four of them spend a lot of time together.

Dylan, Levi, and Zane have arrived and we're just waiting for… Ryder walks in last. He waits by the door for a moment and I wonder what he's doing, until I see he's joined by a woman. Seeing Ryder with a woman is certainly not an unfamiliar sight, but when I get a look at his face, I about pass out. "Oh my god," I whisper and Cole looks at me in confusion and follows my gaze. "Ryder's in love."

Cole smiles and nods, and I can understand now why I thought he looked happier than I've ever seen him – because he is. Ryder introduces me to Tessa, smiling proudly the whole time, and doesn't take his hands off of her. It's clear that the guys have all done a lot of changing over the years. It's obvious not only in their interactions with one another, but in the way they are with the women they love too. It makes me ache with a desire to have that too. I wonder just how much Cole has also changed over the years; and realize it's likely significant, because I've changed too. And we're likely better people. But the million dollar question is, are we merely good friends, good companions, or could we have the potential for something more?

I've missed this group, this dynamic, and this emotional place I'm in when I'm with this gang. It feels so natural, so easy. I know I could fit in with all of them once again, and I find myself startled that I'm longing for a chance.

Alarmed at my thoughts I'm grateful when we place our orders and Cole breaks my train of thought. "Seriously, man, if you don't stop glowering at me, I'm going to punch the look off your face," he says staring at Ryder.

Ryder crosses his arms and tries to look threatening, but the curve of his lips give away his true emotions, "I went over to your place like three times and you weren't there," Ryder says.

"So," Cole says and Ryder frowns deeper.

"So, I was worried about you, alright?" Ryder says exasperated.

"Aww, having a woman has made Ryder get all soft," Zane says teasingly and it generates a growl and a curse from Ryder.

"You've been busy lately," Cole says gesturing to Tessa. "I've just been giving you space. It's not a big deal. What were you worried about anyway?"

Ryder's eyes swing to mine and then back to Cole and the reason is clear, "I just was, okay. You had said you would be coming to the gym to work out and didn't...we used to walk over together all the time...I hadn't seen you in a while... I don't know... fuck, maybe I am getting all sissy like." He points to Tessa, "This is your fault!"

"I think it's sweet, baby," she says to him and Ryder leans toward her and kisses her mouth.

"So, what brought you to Arizona, Tatum? Just a visit, or something else?" Rowan asks me from across the table.

"I had an art showing at a gallery in Tempe. Since I hadn't been back in a while, I thought I'd make a week vacation out of it."

"What kind of art showing?" Dylan asks me.

"Um, mine actually."

"Yours? That's awesome," Zane says.

"Thank you. It's my first gallery exhibit and first stop on a tour. This one here in Arizona is the first stop on the tour and I'm heading to a few other locations as well. California is up next. It's exciting."

"Congratulations," Jax says and murmurs of congratulations circulate the table.

"Thank you" I tell them genuinely.

"What kind of things do you paint?" Levi asks me curiously.

"All kinds of things. People, landscapes, items, whatever makes me feel inspired to pick up a brush. I have all kinds of different paintings on display for the tour, a couple different themes as well."

"Can we still go see them?" Tessa asks kindly.

"Yes, they are on display through the rest of the week until they wrap and ship them to California."

"You know...if you ever need a model to paint, I know the perfect person for you," Levi says.

"Is that right?"

"Yes, it's-"

"If you nominate yourself, I'm going to laugh my ass off," interrupts Ryder.

"Especially because I would be the better subject for sure," Zane adds.

"You?" Levi scoffs. "I don't think so. My cheekbones are to die for."

"My muscles are bigger than all of yours," Ryder says making Tessa and everyone laugh and of course he flexes to prove it.

"Yeah well, I bet she would kill to paint my eyes," Jax says with a laugh.

"Oh for sure," Rowan says, "but your ego would probably overshadow them."

Cole and I laugh as everyone argues about who has the better feature, and when our food is delivered it doesn't stop the conversation. The atmosphere is fun, the food is great, and the company entertaining. Just as our plates start being removed and Lily begins entertaining us by dancing to the music being played over the speakers, there's a loud commotion.

"Where the fuck is he? I know the bastard's here."

A few of the guys look toward the door where the loud voice is yelling and we all look around in confusion. "They told me at the gym they're here. I want to see him now. Get off me! No, let me go."

"What the hell?" Zane says as he stands from his seat.

Cole stiffens beside me and he and Ryder lock eyes. Silent communication passes between them, and my eyes volley back and forth trying to understand what is going on.

"Cole!" The voice begins yelling. "Cole Russell, get your goddamn ass out here right now. You need to get training right this fucking minute."

"You've got to be kidding me." Jax says in frustration and looks at Cole in question, who shakes his head. Jax disappears as Rowan looks on in distress.

"Cole?" I look at him as I see him stand from his chair. "What's going on?"

"Cole, you don't need to deal with this. Stay here," Ryder says and Levi and Zane echo his statement.

"No, he's my problem, I'll handle it."

"The fuck he is," Ryder growls.

"It's fine." Cole looks at me and I'm shocked at the weariness and defeat I see in his eyes. "I'll be right back. Wait here."

Cole disappears and I hear some more yelling but can't make out what's being said now. I have no idea what's going on, but the guys look stressed and Jax still hasn't returned. "Who is that? What's going on?" Most of the guys look away from me, either not comfortable with sharing something that is between them, or not wanting to divulge Cole's business, I'm not sure. "Zane, who's yelling out there?"

"Don't worry, Tatum. It's nothing new, unfortunately. Cole and Jax will handle it."

"Handle what?"

"It's Jax's father and Cole's trainer, Jerry. He's been drinking a lot lately and these incidences are becoming more and more normal," Rowan says and when I look at her in surprise she shrugs, "I would want to know too."

"Thank you," I tell her and she nods.

"Why they put up with his shit at all, I don't understand. Especially Cole. We've been trying to find out for years why he keeps putting up with Jerry's shit, but we cant get anything from him. Maybe you would have more luck than we have, Tatum," Ryder tells me.

"Does he always talk to Cole like that?"

Ryder nods, "He talks to all of us that way anymore. He's always drunk half the time. It's amazing he can train Cole at all. It certainly can't be quality training and I have suspicions that he spends more time degrading him than anything else, but still Cole won't walk away. I don't get it. He's a great fighter, but with better training, he'd be unbeatable."

"Speaking of fighting, are you going to come and watch his fight?" Levi asks me.

"His fight?"

"Yeah. Tomorrow night. You're going right?"

He has a fight tomorrow night and he didn't tell me? Maybe he doesn't want me to go. He probably didn't ask because he doesn't want me to feel obligated to attend. "Oh yeah, I can't believe that is tomorrow night already. Where and what time is it again? I know he said, but I completely spaced it."

"This one is at the main Top Team Sporting Center complex in Phoenix. Cole's round is supposed to start at 8PM."

"I'll definitely be there. I'm looking forward to it."

"Yeah, we are too. He's up against a tough opponent, but if he concentrates and shows no mercy, he's got it in the bag. Should be a good fight."

Before I can comment, Cole returns to the table. His demeanor is distressed and tense. "Is everything okay?"

He nods, but won't make eye contact. He must be gritting his teeth because his jaw muscles keep tightening and releasing, evident on the side of his face. And then I see his blood vessel in his forehead pulsing. I'm not sure what to do, what to say, I don't even understand what's going on.

Everyone disperses and I wave goodbye at everyone and receive a few hugs and "nice to meet you's." As Cole and I walk back to his place, I can't help but take his hand into my own, "I don't know what happened, but I know whatever it is, you're upset about it. Can I help in any way?"

He looks down at my face and holds my gaze for a moment. He takes a deep breath and I can see some of the stress leave his face. He holds up our joined hands and looks at them, "This helps. Thank you."

I give his hand a squeeze and don't let go all the way to the parking lot of his apartment complex. "Thank you for dinner. I'm going to see you tomorrow, right?"

He nods and I can see the muscles in his throat working as he swallows, "Yeah, your last day."

"Yes," I practically whisper, an ache in my chest at the thought.

"I have something I have to do tomorrow night, but I can stop by your place to take you to lunch tomorrow, would that work for you?"

"Yes. That sounds great."

"Okay, good night, Tatum." He brushes the hair away from the side of my face and places a soft kiss on my cheek. As the hair from his chin tickles my face, it gives me chills and I want so much to kiss him. To kiss the stress and worry right off of his face and out of his body. I want to throw myself in his arms and pretend that I'm not leaving. I want to feel his body pressed against mine, feel the way he used to love me one last time. I want to be with him intimately, close my eyes and pretend that we have all the time in the world.

Instead, I smile, nod, and whisper good night.

I watch in my rearview mirror as he stands there and watches me drive away. Thoughts of turning back around enter my mind, but I continue on to my hotel. Once there, I pick up the phone and dial.

"Tatum, hi. I was wondering if I would hear from you tonight."

"Hi Blaine," I sigh, not sure how to begin to say what I need to.

"How was your day today? Did you do anything fun?"

"Blaine, I will always be grateful for everything you've done for me. You helped me work through my problems when I was frightened and scared in a new place. You helped me come to grips with the loss of Hope and to learn to love myself again, or at the very least to take the first steps on the path to forgiving myself. I can't ever repay you for that."

"Tatum-"

"No, please let me finish. I believe that you came into my life exactly when I needed you most. I don't know, and can't imagine what I would have done if I hadn't had your guidance, acceptance, and strength these last several years. But, Blaine, I'm ready to move on now. Being here has made me realize that my heart and soul aren't ready to be given to you, maybe I'll never be able to give them again to anyone else, I don't know, but it's not fair to you for me to continue this relationship any longer."

"Tatum," he sighs wearily, "we can discuss this when you get home. When you're away from there. You're surrounded with a history that you have fond feelings for and it's all likely overwhelming and confusing you. And it makes sense that you would have some confusion over the future given the past staring you in the face right now. It's the first time you've been back to Arizona since your loss and honestly, I've been waiting for this."

"No, Blaine. You're wrong. Being away from here isn't going to change how I feel."

"I think it will, and we can talk about this when you get back like I suggested. We will have a healthy conversation, evaluate your visit, and determine where exactly these feelings are coming from. I'll see you when you get here, okay?"

"Good bye, Blaine. Thank you…for everything."

I can hear him start to say something else, but I press the end button on my phone and then shut it off completely. As I change into my pajamas and wash my face, I feel lighter than I have in…I don't even know how long.

Maybe on one hand Blaine is right, maybe being here and remembering my history is making me resurface feelings that will fade away when I leave. Maybe I'm just caught up in being around Cole again and remembering what used to be. I don't know. What I do know is that I want to be in a position where I'm free to find out.

CHAPTER ELEVEN

Cole

I'm nervous about tonight's fight and I'm not sure why. I haven't been able to shake the feeling that something is about to hit the fan. Jerry showing up in a drunken rage like he did last night certainly doesn't help – it's only managed to emphasize the feeling. My initial reaction was to freeze, I could feel the panic welling in my throat, closing it, making me want to run and hide. I hate that I allow him to make me feel weak and worthless, but he owns me. At one time I fought against it, still tried to push him and remember I had rights, but little by little he's worked at and succeeded in stripping the old me away. If I'm honest, I just quit trying and let him. Giving in was easier than fighting a losing battle.

Surprisingly, things went easier and even better with Jerry than I initially expected last night. All it took was a threat from Jax to call the police and have him arrested for drunken disorderly conduct to get him to calm down and listen. I know Jax had no idea why Jerry showed up there and caused a scene – no idea what Jerry would get out of doing something like that. But I do. It was all a charade for my benefit – him trying to prove a point. He wanted me to remember that he's always there, always watching, always making sure that I'm holding up my end of the deal. The thing is, and what scared me last night, is that I'm not. I'm not holding up my end of the deal at all – not since I've been with Tatum. Fortunately, we got him out of there, but I know that I'll end up being the one to pay for Jax's words with Jerry over his antics as if it's all my fault.

I've been both looking forward to and dreading seeing Tatum all day. She's only here for a matter of hours and then she's leaving.

Gone from my life again. This time though, maybe I can get her to share her phone number with me, keep in touch. Just thinking that makes me shake my head and laugh at myself. I keep having this delusional thought that Tatum and I can be friends with each other when I know that isn't possible. We can never be *just* friends.

Grabbing my keys from the table by the door, I turn to leave so I can pick Tatum up from her hotel for our lunch date when there's a knock on the door. Frowning that someone is going to delay my plans, I swing the door open and quickly feel my expression change to confusion when I see Tatum standing there. "Hey. I was just leaving to pick you up. What are you doing here? Did I confuse our plans?"

"I just…can I come in?" she asks and the look on her face makes me step back to let her in immediately.

"Of course." When I do so, she walks inside a few steps and I shut the door. When I turn to her, she's simply standing there staring at the floor. She's biting her lip and picking her nails, plus her breaths appear to be coming quickly. Worriedly, I ask, "Tatum, what's wrong? Has something happened?"

"Yes. Yes, something's happening. I'm leaving tomorrow," she says and then stops and looks at me. Then she closes her eyes and swallows heavily. I'm not sure what she's thinking, but whatever it is, her demeanor is making my chest ache. "And I find that I'm feeling torn, Cole. Part of me is ready to go home. This week has been…unexpected, sad, and draining, yet somehow it's also been exciting, promising, and fun. The truth is, a part of me, and I think it's a bigger part, hurts at the thought of leaving – thinking about going home makes me want to cry." She clutches her chest when she says this as if she's feeling pain right now.

I remain still and silent. Doing so makes my chest burn and my throat ache. Can she hear it? Can she hear that inside my chest my heart is screaming for her to stay? It's bloody, bruised, and bleeding from trying to get my attention; it's begging me to voice the feelings it holds trapped inside. It wants me on my knees, to crawl and scrape my way to her feet and beg her forgiveness, to tell her that since she left I've been a shell of the man that I used to be. The man that I was before came from knowing her, from loving her. Since I lost her, I rarely smile, I hardly laugh, and I have trouble finding and seeing the goodness around me anymore. It's gone. But after just a couple days with her, I remember what it's like to *feel* again. I don't want her to leave, god I don't, but I can't ask her to stay either. She can't.

"When I was with you last night, I wanted so badly to throw my arms around you and kiss you," she says and touches her lips as if she can feel my lips there against hers. She glances behind her and then begins walking backwards and I follow her mesmerized. "I wanted to press my body against yours, lose myself, and remember what it was like to feel passion again. The kind of passion we had before…" she doesn't finish that thought, but I know what she was going to say. Before we lost Hope. We were never able to get enough of each other before that. "I broke up with Blaine," she blurts out and I stop walking, and instead watch, and wait. "I can't be with him when…when my heart still belongs to someone else." She opens the door to my bathroom, looks inside and then closes it. She moves toward the next door and her words have me so stunned it takes a moment for me to realize her intent.

"I want to remember, Cole." With those words she swings open the door to my bedroom.

"Tatum!" I say, "Wait!" But she's not listening.

"I don't know when I will get the chance again, and this morning when I woke up, I thought to myself, what do I have to lose? I want to be-" her next two words, "with you," are spoken softly because her eyes are already taking in the room around her and it's clear she can't comprehend what she's seeing.

"What?" She spins little by little taking in the room. My mind is reeling. I don't know how I'm going to explain this to her. I don't know what I'm going to say. How can I explain that every wall of my room is covered with pieces of her art? That she's never been far from me all this time. I've always kept abreast of where she's been, what she was doing – as much as possible - I demanded it. When I could, I had pieces of her work sent to me through a contact at her school. Discarded homework pieces, or when the school would have mini showings and make them available for purchase, I was sent some. I've even bought some from a gallery before when I was told they were there. Anything I could get, I obtained and tried to imagine her painting each one. I did anything I had to for a piece of her. When she was telling me about her school dictated showings and sales, I made sure I didn't react, already knowing full well about them.

"I don't…I don't understand." She looks at me and her eyes are huge in her face. Tears threaten to fall and disbelief paints her face red. "How? How do you have these?"

"Tatum…" I walk toward her with my hands out as if she's a deer I'm trying not to frighten.

"Cole!" she says loudly, her voice shaking, a tear rolling down her cheek. "Cole, I don't understand." She keeps turning around and around, and I imagine maybe she feels as if she's seeing things.

"I know," I tell her because what else can I say?

"No. That's not good enough." She stops and stares at me wide-eyed and the look in her eyes could bring me to my knees if I let myself drown in it. "How do you have these?" She enunciates each word as if speaking them takes great effort.

"I can't-"

"NO!" she screams. "NO! No, goddamn you. How the fuck do you have these paintings? This one," she runs to the side of my room and points to a painting of a vase holding red roses, "I painted this not long after I started at art school. And this one," she points to an abstract painting that she titled chaos on a label taped to the back. I could almost feel the turmoil in her heart and mind when I received this one and pictured her painting it. Hair piled on top of her head, brow furrowed, random paint coloring her face and arms, oblivious to the world around her. It made me hurt for her in a way that was almost debilitating. "I painted this one a couple years ago. It was selected by an art gallery to display for sale, it sold quickly and-" her voice cuts off. She spins around and looks at me, shaking her head; the look in her eyes rips me to shreds – betrayal, confusion, and anger.

"Explain this to me, Cole! Right now! I don't understand!"

"I know. I know you don't. But, I can't. I can't explain. I'm sorry." She runs to me and slams her fists against my chest.

"No! No! You don't get to do that. You don't get to keep this form me. Not this. Not anymore. You don't get to make me more confused that I already am." Her fists hit me in the chest over and over and over again as she yells, as she cries. I'm not sure that she's even aware of the fact that she's now sobbing. I just let her. I hold the top of her arms and ride it out. I let her hit me; I let her take out her anger, bitterness, and feelings of betrayal, as she should. It's been a long time coming.

"It's okay. I know. I know," I whisper to her like a mantra over and over until her forehead rests on my chest, and while gripping handfuls of my shirt in her hands, her knees buckle. Sinking to the floor with her in my arms, I hold her tight and rock her back and forth as she lets it out.

Eventually her cries stop, and a while after that she pulls away from me and her face is smeared with tears, her eyes convey loss and confusion. I wipe away what I can with my thumbs and we stare at each other, words not passing between us, yet so much is said. I tuck her hair behind her ear on one side and kiss her cheek, closing my eyes at the feel of my cheek rubbing against hers. When I pull away, we hold eye contact. I don't know who moves first, and I don't care, I just know that my lips are suddenly on hers and she's kissing me back. She moves her lips against mine quickly, and through her kiss I feel passion laced with anger and longing. It's in the way she begins to cry silently as she kisses me, the salt from her tears lingering on her tongue. It's in the way she clutches my shoulders in desperation, and in the way she presses her body against mine.

Pulling back from me, she scrambles to straddle my lap, then finds my lips again. Her tongue slides against mine her lips silently asking for more. Her hands find the bottom of my shirt and she tugs, I move away from her and hold her gaze as she moves the shirt over my head. Her eyes scan my torso and turn heated, when she spies a tattoo on my left side over my ribs, the heat wanes and her eyes fill with tears again. "I didn't see this the other night," she says.

"It was dark, and my shirt wasn't up high enough," I shrug.

She takes a finger and traces Hope's name, then leans down and kisses each letter. When she sits back up, she stares at me before slowly removing her own shirt. Her breaths come quicker now; her breasts straining against the white lace bra she's wearing with each inhale and exhale. She watches me as she moves her hands behind her back and unsnaps her bra. With deliberate slowness now, she slides one strap down her shoulder and then the other before pushing it aside.

She doesn't need to say a word, what she wants, what she needs, is evident. Taking my face in her hands, she kisses me on the lips, and presses her body against mine. I inhale sharply and moan at the feeling of her skin on mine. My mind, my heart, my soul, and my hands are full of her.

The rest of our clothes quickly follow the others and when we are bared to each other it's as if we're in a race. Before I can barely blink, she's astride me again, has me in her hand and I'm inside of her. For a moment we simply allow ourselves to feel our connection.

Taking her face in my hands this time, I tell her what's on my heart, "You've always been with me, Tatum. These paintings...well you've always been on my mind and in my heart. Always."

A tear falls down her cheek and I lean forward to kiss it away. When we begin to move, every touch is weighted, every push and pull ignites, and every stroke and cry marks my body with a memory to keep with me always. I feel everything - her skin like silk as it rubs against mine, the ends of her hair as it tickles my chest, the carpet and her nails as they scrape my skin, the sweat that begins to bead on our bodies, and the way she feels while connected to me.

When we finally climax, we do so together, my shudders of ecstasy are breathed into her mouth combining with hers. Long after, I hold her tightly to my chest, scared, worried, and not willing to let go. Eventually she pulls away from me, and I'm relieved when I see there's no regret in her eyes, only contentment.

We spend the rest of our time together naked and on the floor wrapped up in each other. At one point we grab food from the refrigerator and bring it right back to the room and eat it picnic style. While I know she has questions, she doesn't ask them. Instead, she points to each painting and tells me their story. What inspired her to paint it, why she chose the colors she did if it isn't obvious, the grade she received for the assignment and anything else that may go along with it. I soak it all up, all the while reveling at the fact that she's here with me again.

When the room begins to darken with the setting sun, I glance at the clock and realize I've run out of time. "Tatum, I'm sorry but I have to go. I have plans I can't get out of, but you said your plane doesn't leave until late morning tomorrow, right?"

"That's right," she says, her voice sounding gravelly from the tears she shed earlier.

"Can I take you to the airport? Maybe grab an early breakfast with you?"

She swallows and nods. "Yes," she whispers and I wince at the pain laced in a single word.

We get dressed in silence, the weight of her imminent leaving heavy between us. I walk her to the door, pull her into my arms and kiss her. "I'll see you in the morning."

"See you soon," she says with a wink and leaves.

I take a moment to gather myself before grabbing my gym bag and the things I need before heading out the door behind her. While driving to the arena where my fight will be held, I try to transition my thoughts from Tatum to the fight ahead of me. Turning on some music, I use it to help me switch my headspace.

I'm barely through the door of the dressing rooms when Jerry is on my case. "It's about fucking time you get here, boy. You were supposed to get here fifteen minutes ago. I was about to send someone to find you."

"After fifteen minutes? That's ridiculous," I tell him even thought it's pointless.

"Get dressed smart ass. You need to get warmed up."

Ducking my head, I move to the bathroom and change my clothes quickly. When I exit my hands are wrapped with tape, and I start jumping around and shadow boxing to get the blood moving through my veins.

"There's no reason you shouldn't win this fight. He may be bigger and stronger, but you're smarter. Your win will mean a huge payout and I need this. You need this," Jerry says gleefully.

And therein is the reason he lined up this fight against Bruce 'Bulldozer' Jennings to begin with. It never should have been done. He's been fighting longer than me, and his opponents have been on a level I haven't reached quite yet – they are also in a higher weight class. I'm good, and I'm almost there, but I'm not yet. He arranged it because the money if I beat someone a weight class ahead is twice the usual sum. How he got them to agree to that, I'll never know. But,

I'm not an idiot, and I know Jerry's dealings and the arrangements he makes aren't always on the up and up. It's not like I can say a goddamn word about it though, he made sure of that, and I agreed to it all.

Someone ducks their head in to tell us it's time for me to make my way to the ring. There were other events before mine, some really good cards too, even though Jax and the guys aren't fighting tonight. I'm actually glad since I would have missed them – well except for Jax. He's always a headliner, which drives Jerry fucking crazy, so of course it always makes me happy. It's the little things.

As I begin making my way down the hallway toward my designated arena entrance, I almost smile when speaking of the devils I see Jax, Levi, and Ryder up ahead. They are watching me intently, no doubt worried about what's about to go down. They each tried asking me about this fight one by one when it was announced, all disagreeing with the match up. I nod at each of them doing my best to convey assurance, but it doesn't seem to work.

Just as I'm about to pass them, someone pushes out in front of Ryder and I do a double take before I stop completely. Panic. Panic runs through me like fire and my heart beats double time. Tatum. Tatum is here. "Tatum? What are you doing here?"

"Levi told me about your fight tonight," she says and I glare at Levi who looks surprised by this statement. Putting his hands up he says, "Dude, I mentioned it at dinner. I had no idea she didn't already know about it. You played me," he says to Tatum and she ignores him.

"You can't be here," I tell her. "Please go. Now. I'll call you when this is over, okay? I promise, but I need you to go now."

"What? No. I want to see your fight, Cole."

Terror runs through me and I glance at Jerry. He was walking ahead of me, and I'm thankful that he is talking to someone and has no clue that I've stopped several steps behind him. "Tatum, please," I plead. Jerry can't see her. He can't. And then, my blood runs cold.

"What the hell is going on?"

"Tatum," I whisper. "Go." Then I look at Jax in panic, "Jax?" He nods, but before he can make a movie Jerry asks again, "Who the hell are you talking to? A woman?"

I turn and make sure Tatum is behind me, blocking her from view. "It's no one," I tell him and try not to wince at the lie. She's everything. She's fucking everything. I silently tell her I'm sorry in my mind.

"Did you seriously bring one of your fucks here, boy? You know how I feel about that. You need to keep your head in the fucking fight, not on your dick."

"My head is where it needs to be, don't worry," I tell him and after looking over my shoulder at Tatum, I look toward Ryder and Jax and again beg, "Please," I say soft enough that Jerry can't hear me, but loud enough that they can. "Keep her away from him."

Ryder and Jax both stare hard at me, and I know they each have questions that will likely come later. The great thing about them though is that they know now isn't the time and they won't hesitate to do what I ask for a second. I want to keep Tatum away from Jerry's eyes, at any cost. "Please," I ask them again and they each nod immediately, "You got it," Jax says.

"Don't worry," Ryder says. "Go."

I nod and don't look at her again before I walk away. I can't. God, she shouldn't be here. I don't want her to see this. I don't want him to see her. He can't see her.

When I reach the door, I'm announced, and I make my way down the aisle. I barely pay attention to the music Jerry selected to play as I walk, or the cheers around me. It's loud and thundering and usually pumps me up even more, but right now, nothing can do that. I just want this to be over.

When I'm finally in the octagon, they don't waste any time getting the fight started, immediately announcing each of us and stating our statistics. I wince when the ten-pound difference between "Bulldozer" and I is announced. I had to agree to fight someone in a weight class higher than my own, and looking at him up close and personal I'm regretting that decision. He's built like a brick shit house. Fact is, Jerry does what he wants and I just go along for the ride, hardly paying attention, although this time I should have. Too late to back out now.

Jumping around in my corner, I try to focus. From the side, standing out from the crowd, I hear Ryder shout, "Alright, let's do this. Head in the game. Bring him down, Cole." Glancing toward him, I see him standing with the other guys. All of them are standing and have their arms crossed over their chests, and right between the intimidating line they make is Tatum. The sight makes my movements falter and I hear Jerry question it and curse something behind me. Ignoring him, my thoughts don't stray from her as Bulldozer and I meet in the middle and bump fists, wishing each other, "good luck."

I'm distracted by her presence – knowing her, she refused to go. Apart from carrying her out over their shoulders, they would have tried and said anything to get her to go. The look on her face was pure fury. Squeezing my eyes shut quickly, I do my best to push her from my mind for now. Jerry won't chance looking over there with Jax among them, so she's safe for now. The bell rings and Bulldozer and I begin circling each other. Round and round we go until finally we each make the first move – at the same time. We both start throwing combinations, neither of us landing any significant blows. When we back away from each other, my nerves have finally been shaken and I'm in the zone now.

My strategy going in was to take him to the ground as soon as I could because I had been told, and saw when I reviewed one of his fights, that he's really good on his feet. It's apparent to me that his take down defense has improved drastically because he's defending each of my attempts well – I can't get him to the ground. After a few more times trying to take him down, we clutch each other against the wall, until the referee separates us. He immediately comes at me with a flurry of punches, one grazes me, and when I feel something slide down my face I can't tell if it's sweat or blood. I also throw combinations of my own again, landing a couple, but I don't think it's done any damage. It seems to be a slugfest this first round, and the round itself seems to be taking forever to end. I attempt once more to try to take him down, because I'm much better at grappling than boxing. It doesn't work, so this time, I go for his knee, but he lands a solid to my face during the attempt making blood explode from my face and fly in the air and splatter on the mat. I'm pretty sure my nose is broken. Sniffling and trying to ignore it, I stand up, just as the bell rings.

As soon as I head back to my corner and Jerry, he starts in on me. "What the fuck is this shit? This isn't fighting. This is you getting your damn ass kicked. Stop being a goddamn pussy for once in your miserable life and get this done already. This isn't the kind of fighting that gets us paid, son."

God, I hate him. "Are you not watching the same damn fight? I've tried taking him down and haven't been successful."

"I've seen poor ass attempts." He starts telling me what I need to do, mixed with insults like usual while at the same time sopping up the blood from my face and applying cold steel to reduce swelling where he can. I grunt when he shoves gauze up my nose in an attempt to stop the blood flow before I go back out. As soon as he pulls it back out so I can resume the fight, I feel a couple drops on my upper lip and know immediately, his attempts to stop the blood flow didn't work. I can hear the guys yelling encouragement from their places ringside, a female voice among them standing out from the rest. "Come on, Cole. You've got this." I almost smile – almost.

As we head out for round two, when the bell rings, I begin by trying to kick Bulldozer in his legs several times hoping they'll weaken from the strikes enough for me to finally take him the hell down. He continues to come forward, swatting off my strikes like flies, and lands another combination which stuns me. I see double for a moment.

"What the fuck was that, Cole. Shake it off. Shake it the fuck off, you bastard. I thought you were better than this, maybe not."

I actually manage to chuckle without humor at his less than supportive words although I don't know how. I feel pain. My right eye begins to swell up, and I can't tell if it's my head, my heart, or my nose, but I'm pounding every-goddamn-where in rhythm to my heartbeat. I try not to let it distract me and throw some haymakers trying to land something – anything. When I connect, it's not promising because it doesn't appear to have had much of an impact on Bulldozer. He lands another flurry of shots, and I suddenly realize I'm getting my fucking ass kicked.

I'm bleeding down the side of my face from the top of my eyebrow; my nose is broken, my right eye is hard to see through and is swelling more and more by the second. Nothing I seem to try is working, he just keeps coming at me again and again, this time throwing shots to my face. Yet another round that feels like it's lasting forever. I'm not going to lie; I just want this over, and over now. I want to talk to Tatum. I want to get this time back from this stupid fight and instead choose to spend it with her. For an insane moment, I even contemplate dropping my arms and walking off. Suddenly, I feel incredibly done. I feel tired. I feel like I can no longer carry this fucking weight on my back anymore. I want to quit – even if it means they carry me out of here.

Bulldozer comes in right then and starts wailing on me. Jerry is screaming, the guys are screaming, but it doesn't matter. I can't defend his strikes; they're coming fast and furious. I cover my head to try and fend off the worst of them and then pull myself into a ball. I'm done.

The referee steps in between us and stops the fight just as the bell rings. I clearly didn't have it in me to fight him tonight – maybe not any night. He is the better fighter and should have won. I'm glad the referee stopped it. "What the fuck was that? You are a piss poor excuse for a fighter. Do you know how much money you've lost me?" He's pissed and embarrassed, but I don't give a fuck. I'm past caring.

After they officially declare Bulldozer the winner, I leave the octagon eager to get back to the locker room so I can see a doctor and take a hot shower. My adrenaline is still pumping, but when it wears off I'm going to be in a hell of a lot of pain. Just as I hit the aisle, Tatum is there. "Cole. Oh my god, are you okay?"

"Tatum," I glare at her with my one good eye. I'm angry, exhausted, and embarrassed that she saw me get my ass kicked. "Why are you here?"

"I said that I wanted to see you fight."

I laugh bitterly, before I remember Jerry and look around quickly to see that he's not here. Not yet. "I don't want you here," I tell her harshly almost wincing at my words. "I thought I made that clear before. Just fucking leave."

She stares at me, her mouth open, and I feel like a dick for my harsh words but know that she'll follow me clear back to the locker room if I don't say them. And that can't happen. "You're an asshole, you know that?" Her eyes well with tears, "I can't believe I thought-"

"Cole! Get the fuck to the locker room," Jerry says from close by startling me. Turning away from Tatum, I hurry to the locker room, my interaction with Tatum making me feel sick.

As soon as I get to the locker room, Jerry starts in on me again, but I head to the shower and use the warm water to drown out his words happy when he leaves the room. Wincing at the stinging sensation each touch of water brings to my injuries, I watch the water turn pink from my blood as it washes down the drain. I keep seeing Tatum's face in my mind, the look of hurt and betrayal at my harsh words. I hate myself.

When I put my street clothes back on, the fight doctor is there to handle my wounds. He works quickly and even gives me some pain meds to take tonight should I need them. For now I down some ibuprofen then sit on the bench, my head in my hands. "You look like you're in pain, you must be replaying the fight in your mind, huh?"

Looking up I find Ryder standing there and I feel surprised. "What are you doing back here?" They always try to avoid Jerry at all costs.

"You've been beat up enough tonight, if Jerry even tries to speak to you again like he did out there, I'll have a few things to say to him."

"I don't need a babysitter."

"I'm not your babysitter, I'm your fucking friend. Deal with it." Saying nothing, I sigh. "What the hell is going on, Cole?"

"I'm pretty sure you saw what everyone else saw. I got my ass kicked."

"I'm not fucking talking about that and you know it. What the hell is going on with Jerry? Why do you let him treat you that way? Talk to you that way? Jax would coach you in a second."

"I know, it isn't about not wanting Jax as a coach."

"Then what is it? And don't tell me to mind my own business because I'm done doing that. God, Cole, the way you looked at us when you saw Tatum here – you were scared. You were scared that Jerry would see her. Why?"

I stare at him and say nothing until he sighs at me. "Ryder, look, I get that you care. I do. And I would tell you if I could, but I can't."

"You can't or you won't?"

"I can't."

"We all know that Jerry has you tied up in some shit. It's the only explanation and we aren't fools. Just tell me what it is so we can help you."

"Ryder-"

"Look, I'm going to do you a solid, because when I needed it, you were there for me. So shut up and listen," I hold up my hands in surrender. "It's fucking time to let go of your pride."

"It's not-"

"Shut up, Cole. That's exactly what it is. You don't trust us? We've been your friends forever. If anyone can help you with this Jerry shit, it's us. The only reason you haven't spoken to us about it is because your pride won't let you. But, it's time, Cole. You need help."

"Ryder-" I say again but he gives me a look that makes me close my mouth.

"I was there Cole, do you remember? I was there when you went through hell with Tatum and losing your child. I saw what that did to you and I thought that you would never get lower than that. But instead of healing and getting better with time, you turned into something unrecognizable. I've sat back and watched you lose yourself – spiral into incredible depths - and I know without a doubt it has to do with that man. The way you just spoke to her out there. Spoke to the woman that I know you love because I can see it. Hell, maybe because I'm in love now I can recognize it easily in others, but I know how you feel about her and how you just were with her?" He sighs and shakes his head. Walking to me, he places a hand on my shoulder and I look up into his face. "All I'm going to say is this and then I'll let you think on it, okay?" I nod. "The distance between you and help, is your pride. Aren't you tired of feeling like this? It's time for you to be the fighter that I know you are. Grow up, and do something about this. Enough is enough."

I nod and don't say a word because I don't think I could if I tried. He's right. I know he's right and finally having someone say that to me, well I think I've needed to hear it.

He pats me on the shoulder a few times and squeezes it, then he clears his throat. Acting like this with me was more girly than he can handle, so he backs up. I smile, then wince when it makes my face hurt, "Thanks for the chat, girlfriend," I tease and he frowns.

"Shut the fuck up," he says with smile. "Now if I were you, I'd go and find that girl of yours. And here's a piece of advice from someone in a new relationship. Get on your knees and don't be afraid to grovel. Got it?"

"Got it."

"Good. Now go, and Cole, we better talk soon."

Nodding, I walk out of the locker room with Ryder, my friend, at my side, my thoughts already moving to Tatum and begging her forgiveness. Not able to wait until morning, when I get in my car, I head to her hotel, not sure how or what I'm going to say, but needing to see her never the less.

CHAPTER TWELVE

Tatum

I cried the whole drive back to my hotel and I honestly can't determine if it's because I'm sad or livid. Am I sad that I've spent the last few days with him, or angry? Angry that I let him get into my head, my heart, or am I sad? Am I sad that I let myself feel something for Cole again? Who am I kidding? I'm livid because I never stopped feeling for him and instead of letting it fade away, I tapped into those old emotions again. Am I sad that I actually thought that perhaps he was feeling things too? Or am I livid because clearly he doesn't?

After being with him today, as I laid in his arms afterward, I let myself daydream. I dreamed that I would go back home, but he would come after me, or beg me to stay. I dreamed that he would tell me that he loves me, and ask me to consider exploring a future with him. I let my stupid heart feel like maybe there could be a future for us. That this week doesn't have to be our last if we didn't want it to – and I knew that I didn't. I let myself think that somehow that beautiful little girl we had managed to bring us together again. How ridiculous it all seems now.

I never expected the reaction I received from him when he saw me at his fight. I know I didn't tell him I was going, nor did he ask me to attend, but I wanted to surprise him. To show him that I care about what he does, that it matters to me. I wanted to see how far he's come, to revel in a world I know he's always loved. I wanted to share part of his life with him. He seemed so angry, so hell bent on getting me out of there. The guys all tried to convince me over and over, telling me I'll make him nervous, or for some reason he was worried about my safety, or that he would lose because he'd only be concentrating on me. It was all bullshit. I could see even they didn't believe the shit they were saying and they were just as concerned about Cole and his strange behavior as I was. So I refused to go. Clearly that was a mistake. And how many others have there been? Jerry let me know that I was one of many. Is that what made Cole angry…is that why he wanted me to leave…didn't want me to find out the truth that way?

Sitting in the chaise by the window I curl up in a ball and swipe at my watering eyes. Curled up like this makes me catch Cole's scent, still on my clothes, on my skin, so I'm out of my seat in a second and in the bathroom stripping. Turning on the water, I let it warm before ducking under the spray and letting it comfort me. After a moment, I grab the soap and lather it, anxious to get any remaining scent of him off of my body. As I wash each part, memories of his lips kissing there, hands brushing, tickling or nuzzling makes me scrub harder and harder.

Tears begin to fall down my cheeks making me curse, "No, dammit. I will not let him do this to me again. Just stop. I've cried enough tears to last me a lifetime over Cole Ryland Russell."

Forcing myself to finish my shower even though a big part of me wants to sink to the bottom and lose myself, I quickly dress and then hook my phone up to a charger deciding some music is a good idea. Scrolling through my playlist I select Birdy's album. I love this music and it also suits my current mood. Unable to sit because of where my mind immediately goes, I begin moving around the room and gathering my things to pack up. Having spent a week in this room, my stuff is all over the place so with methodical movements I fold and pack everything in its rightful place, working hard to turn my thoughts toward my trip home tomorrow, then in a little more than a week, I'll be headed to California for my next gallery showing. This place will be in my rearview mirror.

Cole had asked if he could take me to the airport, so I was going to have him follow me while I returned my rental car, but screw it, I'll handle it myself as soon as I wake up and then call an Uber to take me to the airport. If I know him, he'll show up here tomorrow ready to take me like nothing ever happened tonight, but I don't plan on being here when he arrives. I'm done.

At the thought, my chest aches and a sob gets caught in my throat. I try, I really try to push it aside, but it's too much. Instead, I give in, and I let it all go. The dam breaks open. I rant and rave at a world that it would provide me a second opportunity with the love of my life only to have it be spoiled yet again. I shake my fist at my traitorous heart for falling for him again. I remind my brain that it is smarter than this, and for good measure, remind my emotions they are not in control. Holding my head in my hands, I sob. I sob and somewhere inside of me, while I hate that I'm in this place, I also thank god for it because for years I couldn't feel a damn thing. On some level, I know I've come a long way, and while right now, that doesn't offer me comfort, I know later it will. And so I hang onto that, and I stand up, and I wipe my face, and I decide to do what I always do, I keep moving forward.

There's a loud knock at the door and it makes me jump. I remain still a moment thinking maybe it's just a kid in the hallway fooling around, but there's a knock again. Looking out the peephole I am shocked to see Cole standing there, and it's not just his presence that shocks me, it's how horribly beat to hell up he is. My hand immediately moves to the handle to let him in, to ask if he's okay, to offer comfort, but I stop. Dropping my hand, I step back. Letting him in will only make us repeat the same cycle and I don't want to play this game anymore.

"Tatum, it's Cole. I know you're in there. I can hear your music playing." I remain still, not saying a word. "Tatum, please let me in. I'd like the chance to explain." He knocks on the door again several times before I hear him curse and sigh. "Tatum, I'm not leaving. I will stay right here and keep knocking every five minutes until you answer the door. I'll stay here all night if I have to. I don't have anywhere else to be. I'd hate to have to break the door down, but I will." I jump when I hear something hit the door that isn't a knock, and then there's the sound of him sliding down the door to sit on the floor. "Tatum, please."

Placing both my hands on the door, I fight with myself. Do I really want to leave things like this with him? I've left here once an absolute mess and I don't want to do it again. I am stronger than this. It doesn't matter what he says; I still get to make a decision that is right for me. And, besides, I don't want to always wonder what would have happened or what he would have said if I had just opened the door. I want closure this time around; if nothing else I need that. I deserve that – damn what he needs. So, after he knocks again, keeping his promise to do so every five minutes, I open the door. He falls into the doorway immediately, not expecting it to open, but he's on his feet immediately and walks inside. His large frame immediately takes up the space and I step back and cross my arms over my chest. "Thank you," he says.

"You look like shit."

"I know," he says with a smile that's actually more of a grimace given the pain he has to be in. For some reason that only manages to piss me off.

"What do you want, Cole? I let you in, so say your piece and then go."

"I just – I want to apologize for earlier."

"So apologize. And then leave."

"Please don't be like that."

"You don't get to tell me how to be. Not after the way you spoke to me. I've never been so humiliated. And after…after what had just happened between us hours before." I fade off not wanting to think about it.

His head falls and he squeezes the bridge of his nose between his fingers, "Tatum, I'm sorry for the way I spoke to you earlier, I really am. I know you don't understand, but I was acting that way because I was nervous. I didn't want you around Jerry."

"Why? What does Jerry have to do with anything? Is this because of the way he acted? The guys said at dinner that he's always like that. In fact, they said they don't know why you put up with it. So what's the deal with him?" And there it is. The look on his face that tells me exactly what he's about to say – in some ways I still know him well. "Don't," I beat him to the punch, "Don't you dare. If you even think about telling me again that you can't tell me anything, I will lose it. Because if that's the case then why the hell are you even here? I'm not playing this game with you anymore, Cole, do you hear me? I'm done. Clearly whatever secret it is that you're keeping, it's more important than anything else to you, you've made that clear. But you know what? Hear me when I say this. You're a liar."

"A liar? How?"

"At Hope's grave, when you told me that the reason everything happened five years ago between us was because you were saving me, I said that maybe I didn't want to be saved. Do you remember what you said to me?" He nods his head, but doesn't speak. "You said life can be taken so quickly, so easily. And that being alive is a gift. You said that being alive and living our lives is the only way that we continue to keep Hope alive. But you know what the funny thing is, Cole? I've been with you for a few days and even I've seen during that time, that whatever this is that you're doing…it's not living at all. You're going through the motions, you're living your life for someone else, you're not living it for you, or for her, and so you are nothing but a hypocrite."

"Tatum-"

"No. I'm done. I don't have anything else to say to you. Take your secrets and go."

"Tatum," he sighs, "I don't want to leave like this."

"Do you know, that I actually had it in my head that maybe we could try again? Can you believe how stupid that is? Go ahead. Laugh," and I take my own advice and start laughing. I start laughing so hard that tears start rolling down my face and I bend over at my waist. "Oh god, it's so funny really. Stupid Tatum mistakes a pity fuck for love and the possibility of something more. I can't believe I'm so dumb for you."

"Don't say that, that's not what that was."

"You don't give a shit about me, Cole. GET OUT! GET OUT! GET OUT!"

He walks to me and grabs my upper arms, shaking me in frustration, "No! I will not leave like this. You've got it all wrong."

I knock his arms off of me and smack him across the face. Hard. "I'm DONE with this. I'm DONE with you. All you've EVER cared about is yourself. I'll admit, you had me going there, I actually believed that maybe I had it all wrong. I mean, I remember, boy do I remember, when you told me that you couldn't handle my depression. That you couldn't handle my unhappiness, and that you couldn't live that way anymore. On one hand you say those things to me, and those are my memories of you. Then I come here and you say that losing me killed you. You say you lose yourself in me. You surround yourself in my paintings, and why is that? So you can remind yourself of a poor choice, a lucky escape, what you threw out of your life? Well I'm putting a stop to that. You aren't going to do this to me again. I'm done with your secrets, and I am done with your lies."

"Those things I said to you, they're true. You are everything to me," he says softly and I'm not sure I heard him correctly, but just the thought makes me laugh again.

"Right. I can tell. Just leave, Cole, for god sakes, let's stop this drama show between us, it's exhausting. Just go."

"Everything…. everything I've done I did it for you."

"I don't want to hear it. I told you to leave!" I yell at him.

He looks me dead in the eyes, "EVERYTHING I've done is for you," he screams and the agony in his voice leaves me breathless.

"What are you talking about?"

"I made a deal. I made a deal to save you."

"A deal?"

"God, Tatum. You were so broken. During those months after we lost Hope, the only time I would see you smile was when I would bring you home books of art from the library. You would go through the pages, your fingers lingering on some pictures, tracing others, a smile on your lips and a light in your eyes. It was the only time I'd see flashes of the way you were before…" His voice fades and he begins to pace and I don't think he even realizes he's doing it. "You know what's funny? I used to hate those fucking books. I brought them home anyway, but I hated them so much because I had long since quit being able to illicit that kind of response from you no matter what I did, no matter what I said, but those books got one every time. Jealous of a book, it's ridiculous, but it was like you couldn't hear me anymore, couldn't see me. I didn't know what to do."

"After one particularly bad night after I came home the third day in a row to find that you hadn't moved for the entire day, I lost it. When I left for work that morning, you were sitting in the chair looking out the window and when I returned hours later, you were in the same spot. Tears running down your cheeks, pain in your eyes. I just," his voice breaks, "like I said, I lost it. I'm ashamed to admit that I couldn't handle it. I left. I left and I went to the gym and I worked out my frustration and pain on the bag. I beat it until I was so exhausted I had to be carried into the locker room. Ryder was pissed of course because that's how he acts when he cares, and he confronted me in the locker room, wanting to know what the hell was going on with me, and so I told him. I told him everything. I hadn't spoken to anyone since losing Hope. I mean, the guys had tried to talk to me, but I couldn't open up. I did that night. I told him everything. How I felt about losing her, how I felt like I didn't only lose her that night, but I lost you too. How you seemed lost. That I couldn't get through to you anymore and the only time you seemed at peace was when you immersed yourself in art."

Tears run down my face. Nothing he's saying is new, I know exactly how I was during those days, but to hear it from his mouth, the way he sounds so broken, lost and in pain, it makes me hurt too. I want to apologize, but it's pointless. I can't take it back, I'm not sure I could even control it.

"But, what I didn't know, Tatum, was that Ryder and I weren't alone in that locker room that night."

"One of the other guys was in there too?"

"No, I wish it had been one of them. If it had they would have done nothing but offer support."

"Then, I don't understand."

"Jerry. Jerry was there and he heard everything. And he started to formulate a plan."

"A plan? What do you mean?"

"I received a call from him a couple days later asking me to meet him. I told him no at first. Jax and him were already starting to have trouble and I was nervous about getting in the middle of anything, but he told me it wasn't about Jax at all, that it was about you. I asked him what the hell he was talking about, but he refused to get into anything over the phone. So I went. I've replayed that moment in my mind over and over through the years. I wonder what would have happened if I had just stayed home - if I had just told him to mind his own business. If I had used my fucking brain and known that nothing good could come from a meeting with Jerry."

"What did he do, Cole?"

He laughs bitterly, "He told me that he overheard my conversation with Ryder, and that he was sorry to hear that you weren't doing well. He told me he could help. That he knew exactly what would make you find yourself again. And so, he offered me a deal. But in exchange… in exchange…"

Dread makes my stomach sour, "In exchange for what? What kind of deal?"

"Tatum, you have to know that I was desperate. I would have done anything to help you. Anything. And he knew that, and he preyed on it, and honestly, I felt like I had no other options." He walks to me and his thumb brushes my cheek, "I was losing you. I could feel you slipping through my fingers and I was worried you might commit-" he breaks off not able to say it, but I know the rest of that sentence. "Every single day, I felt you drift farther away. I couldn't lose you too. I didn't want to live in a world without you in it. It's why I arranged to have our neighbor, Mrs. Heath check in on you. I was afraid that I would come home one day and you… that you…"

I nod my head, because I know what he was afraid of and hell if it doesn't hurt. It hurts so much that I put him through that. I want to comfort him. I want to rub away the red that lingers on his cheek from my strike. I want to hold him and remind him that I'm here, that we got through it, that we'll be okay. But I can't. Because if the bad feeling in my heart and soul is any indication, I'm not sure that we will be.

"Jerry had a connection, a friend at the Institute of Art." And at that statement, it already feels like the walls are closing in. "Jerry called in a favor and asked his friend Trevor to look at your art – I still don't know how he obtained pieces for him to see. They were impressed and with Jerry's urging, they were willing to offer you a scholarship."

Because of Jerry. I got a scholarship at the Institute of Art because of Jerry. Oh god.

"But the scholarship they were offering would have only covered part of the cost. Jerry told me that he would front the rest of the money to make the scholarship a full ride. You would have your schooling, books, meals, room and board, anything that you needed – paid for. You see Jerry received a large inheritance when his dad died. It's part of the reason no one understands his anger over not getting the gym that was left to Jax because he has more than enough money to buy his own. Anyway, he told me that it could be a done deal, but of course, it wasn't coming out of the goodness of his heart."

I'm frozen. I'm not sure if I'm even completely comprehending what he's saying to me right now. I feel nauseous and I sit down in case I need to put my head between my knees.

"He sat down a contract in front of me. It listed all the things he told me would be provided for you at art school, but in exchange… in exchange I basically signed my life over to Jerry."

I'm afraid I'm going to throw up, but I manage to ask, "What does that mean?"

"It means that for five years I've been living my life exclusively for Jerry. At least it feels that way, because I've only been fighting at his direction. When he gave me the contract he said if I agreed to the arrangement, I would have no say in who I fought, when I fought, where I fought, where I trained - nothing. My opinion no longer mattered - all decisions completely managed by Jerry – down to my training times and diet. When I would win a fight, half of my winnings were for me to live on and the other half would go to Jerry until I paid him back for every dollar he fronted for your scholarship. The contract will not be void until I've paid him back in full. For five years, I've been working to pay him back."

"Wait. Stop." I tell him, holding my hand up demanding he stop speaking immediately. My mind is spinning with everything he's just revealed and it takes me a minute to gather my thoughts. "You made decisions for me, for us, without talking to me? You basically forced me into doing this by telling me…by telling me you didn't want me anymore."

"It was a lie. Of course I wanted you. I've always wanted you. I still want you. I couldn't-"

"No. Shut. Up. Cole." I try to calm myself but my breaths begin coming faster and faster. "Jerry came to you with this offer and you just… you just made a decision for both of us," I repeat to myself again because I'm trying to comprehend this.

"It was the only way, Tatum. It was the only way to make you better. Like I said, your art was the only thing getting you through your pain. To me it seemed like the solution, that if you went to school, you would be healed through your love of art. I sacrificed myself for you because there was no other way! I couldn't get through to you. It was the only way to save you!"

"I didn't ask you to save me! I didn't ask you to sacrifice yourself! Hell, Cole. I would never ever ask that of you." Shaking my head in disbelief I stand and I can feel my whole body shaking, "You had no right. You had no fucking right."

"I had every right! I loved you and I would have done anything for you. I've hated every minute of dealing with Jerry, it hasn't been a picnic, but if I had it to do all over again, I would do the same damn thing. It was agony, fucking agony watching you in so much pain and being unable to do a damn thing about it. Finally, finally I was presented with a way to help!" He moves to me and tries to take my hands, but I won't let him. "I can still remember the look on your face when you thought…when you thought I didn't want you anymore. It's haunted me for years. I was gritting my teeth through that interaction so hard that I chipped them. I died inside the day you moved away." He swallows hard and his eyes become glassy, "God, sometimes I would miss you so much it felt like I couldn't breathe. It took me months to wash the sheets we had on the bed we shared. I would keep them in a bag and when the pain became unbearable, I would open it and take a deep breath. The smell of you lingered on them for a long time, and the night I realized it was gone, that I could no longer smell you on them, I got drunk off my ass because I couldn't handle the pain. I kept tabs on you through Trevor as I could because I demanded it through my part of the contract. It's how I obtained your art, so I found a new blanket in a way through them I suppose."

"If you missed me so much why didn't you ever pick up the phone and call me? If it was so hard, why didn't you do something about it? Why didn't you come and see me?"

"I couldn't. The agreement was no contact. I couldn't see you, call you, visit you. And I couldn't tell anyone about the deal. If I told anyone, or saw you, he would cut off the funding and I would automatically be required to add on another five years to the deal. I'm at risk of that by telling you now."

"And after I was already out of school and you didn't have to worry about him cutting off funding? When I graduated? You couldn't trust me enough to talk to me then?"

"Because this is going so well?" He smiles but I'm incapable of finding the humor in this. He's known about this for years, me? I'm still trying to come to terms with it. "Well, I'm still bound by the contract to stay silent, and he could have pulled the plug on my fighting and I needed it. And not just for the money, though I have no idea how I could have earned enough to pay him back without it, but it's because it's all I had. And then so much time had gone by, Tatum. I thought I could hold on a bit longer until the debt was paid. Then maybe life would give me a chance; maybe fate would put us back together again. It was all I held onto - it was my hope. And if you had moved on, well, being reduced to nothing but a blip from your past was a chance I had to take. While I spent each and every day living for you, I hoped and prayed that you were doing the opposite, because moving on from me is what you deserved."

"No, Cole. No. You say that you couldn't do anything about it, but that's not true. Do you think if you told Jax that he wouldn't help you? All this time it never occurred to you that Jerry was taking advantage? Have you verified the amounts he's telling you that you owe? Does he give you receipts? Because guess what, Cole? After finishing my junior and senior year at the Art Institute, I left and went to graduate school at Masters of Fine Arts instead. They offered me a full ride scholarship too, for two years, and their grad school was a specialty program specific to painting, so I switched schools. Did you know that?"

By the look on his face, the fact that he's paled considerably, I'm sure he didn't know that at all. "What?" he asks me, and it's so soft and meek if I hadn't been looking at him I wouldn't have heard it.

"Yeah. I only attended there two years. I can't imagine that after five years you should still be paying off your debt, even if I have no idea of what you make on your fights, but it seems to me that Jerry hasn't been upfront with you. He's manipulated this every step of the way, and you let him. Because you couldn't…what…overcome your pride and ask for help? Admit that maybe this was a mistake? Tell someone what was going on?"

His jaw tightens, "I'll be taking that up with Jerry, count on it. But it was still the right thing to do, Tatum. Four years, two years, it doesn't matter, I still helped take care of you the only way I knew how. I helped put a roof over your head, clothes on your back, food in your stomach, and in the process you got better. I helped do that. Me. My literal blood, sweat, and tears."

He's angry now, but hell, so am I. "What do you want me to say to you, Cole? Thank you? You want me to fucking thank you? YOU RIPPED MY FUCKING HEART OUT! You pushed me away, and all I wanted, all I needed, was you."

"That's not true. It didn't matter what I said, what I did, how I tried to help, I couldn't get through to you. I had no choice but to force you into a decision."

"No, Cole. No. You know what you did? At a time when I needed to be able to make my own decisions, you took them from me. I had just lost a baby, my precious baby. My body failed me; it couldn't do the most basic of things. A choice that wasn't my own, she was taken from me, and then you turned around and made another choice for me too. For what? In the name of love? Is it because after I lost Hope you thought me weak? Incapable of making decisions about my own life?"

"No, you know that's not it. I told you why I did what I did."

"Yes you did. And now I have the right to process this information and make a choice about how I feel about it. That's a *choice* you are not taking from me. You can't."

"Tatum-"

"Cole. Leave. I need time."

"But, we don't have a lot of time, you leave tomorrow."

"I know."

"I don't want to lose you again."

"You don't get to decide how this is going to go for both of us, Cole. Not this time. Please leave."

"Tatum, I just...I need to tell you that I love you. I don't want you to leave me. I've never stopped loving you. Being with you these last few days... I want a future with you. I want to be with you, to love you, to see if we can make something of what's between us. To take back what was taken from us."

"What *you* took from us, Cole."

"Tatum, please."

Walking past him, I move to the door and with tears rolling down my face, I hold it open for him. I feel physical pain at doing so, but I know myself, and I know that I need time to think about this revelation. Part of me is angry, part of me is touched, part of me can't comprehend everything, part of me understands why he made the decision he did, but that's the point, my thoughts are incredibly jumbled. I can't think with him here.

He walks to the door and turns to me. Reaching out, he brushes his thumb against my cheek like he always does, and before I can stop him he kisses me quickly on the lips. "You're right you know, I was a hypocrite. These last five years, I haven't been living. But these last few days with you…these moments with you…I've felt more alive than I have in years. Whatever you decide, thank you for that. Thank you for reminding me what it's like to live and love again. Know that I love you. I will always love you."

Before I can respond, he's through the door and gone. Closing it, I walk toward the bed and collapse, pulling my knees to my chest, I cry. I cry for the woman I was five years ago, lost and broken. I cry for putting Cole through so much pain. I cry for the agony Cole had to feel at making the decision he felt he had no choice in making. I may not like it, I may not agree with it, but on some level, I may be able to understand it in time. I cry for both of us now, because while I love Cole with everything that I am, I understand that sometimes, the pain is too vast and impossible to overcome. That sometimes, love isn't enough.

CHAPTER THIRTEEN

Cole

Leaving Tatum last night felt wrong on so many levels. I had to force myself through the door, and almost went back more times than I can count to beat on the door and beg her to talk to me. I even considered sleeping against her door just so I could stay close to her until she was ready to talk to me again, but figured it was smarter to not press my luck.

I've kept my deal with Jerry a secret for so long that finally revealing it makes me feel a strange mix of dread and freedom. The weight of it became more that I could carry and it was only a matter of time before I broke, I just never expected Tatum would be the receiver of the truth. I never thought I'd see her again, that she'd always be lost in the lie, and now that she's here again, I'm so afraid I've lost her again. The look on her face replays in my mind over and over. Shock, disbelief, anger, pain, and loss – and I put them all there. Part of me wishes I had kept my fucking mouth shut. I feel vulnerable and scared of the repercussions that keeping the truth for so long may have brought, because these kinds of things always have a way of bringing nasty unanticipated consequences.

I've watched the clock all night, sleep impossible. I've paced my small apartment so much that I began driving myself crazy. I knocked on Ryder's door, but he didn't answer. I could use a friend, but the fact is he and all the other guys have tried to be a friend and get me to confide in them for years now. It figures that when I'm ready to talk he wouldn't be there. It's no less than what I deserve. I'm afraid of what they will all think when they hear the truth. I see the confusion and anger on their faces when they watch Jerry boss me around like some little bitch. They hate it, and I think part of them hates me for letting him do it. They've long since given up on me, why should I expect them to care at this point? God, I've done this to myself.

Finally, unable to handle myself any longer I found myself in my bedroom lying on the floor in the exact place Tatum and I had been only hours before. I felt closest to her there, and somehow it helped soothe the foreboding feeling I can't shake. Memories of her run through my mind like an erotic slideshow. Her soft skin sliding against mine, the look in her eyes, the sounds of pleasure that left her mouth, the way she made me feel. I've missed her more than I even realized.

Now, hours later, still lying here, those images fade from my mind, replaced by memories of the first time I broke her heart. Memories I have kept concealed and buried for years before this week. They play over and over like a skipping record, vivid in color and ripe with pain. And for the first time in a long time I begin doubting the decision I made all those years ago. Was she really as bad as it seemed? Could someone else have helped her? Was Jerry's deal really the last resort? Why didn't I tell him to shove his deal up his ass? And then, the darker deeper part of me asks, if was because I really couldn't handle her or the pain of losing Hope any longer. Was having her leave just the easy way out? But I quickly push those thoughts away in anger because nothing about the last five years has been easy. And I recall the significant angst and process I put myself through when I made that decision. I did not quickly pounce on it. I considered other options. It was not an easy decision. I truly believed it was the best and right choice at the time. No one will ever know the many times I questioned myself. In hindsight, knowing what I now know, would I, should I have done the same thing? How can I answer that? Things always look different over time: the known facts are never exact, one's emotions and emotional health is not the same. So much is different five years later. So why do this to myself? It accomplishes nothing. All I know is that she's never, in all this time, been far from my mind or heart even when I did everything I could to leave her and that part of my life in the past. I really did feel like I was saving her, and I put aside my own needs, wants, wishes, and dreams to make sure she had an opportunity to find hers instead. I know the sincerity, the genuine love that enabled me to choose that road. My intentions were the right ones. Of that I am sure.

Looking at the clock again, I sigh seeing it's still not quite a decent hour to go knocking on Tatum's door. She never told me what time her flight leaves, but given the fact we were supposed to have breakfast before she left, I'm assuming it's late morning or early afternoon - plenty of time to talk to her. I have so much I want to say, so much I need to say. I want to tell her what this week has meant for me, how spending time with her and seeing her again has made me feel. I want to affirm that she's not the only one that wishes and hopes for more. I want her to know that my life has been meaningless and empty without her in it, and I'll do anything to have her with me again. I want to get on my knees if need be and beg her to stay, tell her I'll go with her, whatever it takes. I don't only miss her, but I miss the old me. What it was like to be happy, carefree, fun, and sarcastic at times. I will follow her anywhere, do anything I have to in order to repent, I just want her. I know that the love we once felt for each other is still there, I've felt it this week, at times so tangible it was overwhelming. That means something – it has to. I only hope she feels the same way. I can't, no… I *refuse*, to let her go without a fight.

Once it hits a decent hour, I get in the shower and am ready to go in record time. When I hit her hotel lobby, I race through it to the elevators and hit the button over and over again until the damn door finally opens. Pushing the button for the fifth floor I impatiently wait while it feels like it takes forever to get there. When the doors finally open, I race down the hallway and knock on the door, "Tatum!" I yell excitedly, anxious to share my thoughts with her – needing to get them off of my chest. I wait and listen for something to indicate she's coming to answer. "Tatum, please open the door. I want to talk to you, I have so much to say!" I lean my forehead against the door eager to hear her, even if it's to yell at me because she's still mad, but I'm only met with silence.

After incessantly knocking for another several minutes with no response to my pleading and begging, I look around the hallway in frustration and notice a cleaning cart several doors down and get an idea. When I'm next to the cart, I smile and snatch something from it knowing it will help. Looking inside another room that has the door propped open, two cleaning ladies appear inside chatting away and laughing while they make the bed. "Hi," I say and both of their heads swing in my direction in surprise. Smiling coyly while I cross my arms over my chest knowing it makes my muscles push against my shirt, I ask, "I was wondering if one of you could please help me?"

They both smile shyly and nod their heads and I almost sigh in relief, not above using my assets when needed. Luckily the injuries on my face do not appear to divert my plan. They walk out into the hallway when I point down the hall, "I was at my car, placing my luggage in the trunk before I check out, when I realized my phone isn't on me." I pat my pockets absently. "I'm afraid I left it in my room. Would you mind letting me back in really quick so I can check?" They look at each other in hesitation and I smile again, "Please? I promise I will be really quick, my key isn't working, so I don't know if they already disabled it since I told them I'd be checking out this morning, or what." I hold up the random key I took from their cart, smile and shrug, and release a breath when they both smile and nod. Since I'm first out of the room, I discretely place the key back on the cart. I would have used it myself instead of asking for help, but I have no idea if it's a master key. Given the fact they don't stop to grab it and pull one from their pocket instead, it appears I'm correct.

One of them slides the card in the slot and the telltale click sounds. Pushing the handle down, I look past them into the small part of the room I can see and mumble a "thank you." Once I'm through the door, I look back briefly, offer a smile, and then close the door. The woman that unlocked the door widens her eyes just as it closes in her face, "I'll be quick!" I promise. Turning to the room, my gut clenches and I squeeze my eyes closed. Without looking around, I already know she's gone. The room feels hollow, her energy no longer able to be felt.

My mind spins and I feel sick to my stomach.

She's gone.

I've lost her.

Again.

I spin toward the door and grab hold of the handle ready to run after her, and then stop. It's pointless. I could drive to the airport, but I have no idea what time her flight is, or which airline she's on, therefore I'd have to guess which terminal to park at and run around in and do…what? I can't go past security…I can't do… anything. Hell, I don't even have her damn phone number - we never exchanged them, which is so fucking stupid. I have nothing. Nothing to show for the fact that she was even here other than the emptiness that's been left behind.

Turning back toward the room once more, I begin searching it like a madman. Opening every drawer, the closet, ripping the sheets off the bed, looking under the bed, checking by the hotel phone, even doing what I've seen in the movies – using the pen to etch the pad sitting here in case she wrote anything down, but all I've managed to make is an inky mess. She's left nothing behind. Not a hint or clue as to what she's thinking, her whereabouts, itinerary, a note, nothing. There's absolutely nothing to find.

Defeated, I run my hands down my face, sigh and absently sit on the stripped bed. Placing my elbows on my knees, I drop my head, unsure of how to feel or what to think. With burning eyes, I grab the pillow lying at my feet off of the floor and bring it to my face and inhale. Her scent still lingers. I inhale again, flowery, yet sweet, it's intoxicating and completely her. It feels as if my heart cracks in my chest, the absence of her once again almost impossible to contemplate. Just like years ago, all I have is bed linen to hold onto as a reminder - a merged mockery of our past and present. Walking out of the hotel, I take the damn pillow with me, unable to let it go.

Hours later I find myself hitting the bag at the gym. I tried to keep myself distracted. I ran errands I put off during the week, but then I found myself at the airport. All I did was take a couple laps around every terminal perimeter, hoping maybe Tatum would be sitting on a bench, or just walking by, I don't know what I thought but it was stupid. I wasn't above desperate acts. I even went by the gallery before hitting the airport in case she had stopped there. The worst part was when I went home. As I got closer, a crazy thought took hold in my mind – what if she was there waiting for me? My hands tightened on the steering wheel and my foot pressed down on the gas pedal, anxious to get there as fast as I could. When I parked, I jumped out of my car and ran to my apartment door, only to find the doorway as empty as it was when I left it that morning.

Letting myself inside, I tried to nap. Having not slept much the night before, I was certainly tired. I curled up with my new pillow and closed my eyes, willing myself to shut out the nightmare of my reality at least for a little while. The funny thing about dreams though is that sometimes reality finds a way to follow you there too – albeit in twisted ways. In my dream we were mountain climbing.

Tatum used to like to climb Camelback Mountain sometimes on the weekend when we were in college. In my dream she was ahead of me on the path, but no matter how hard I dug my feet into the ground and pushed myself I couldn't catch up. I couldn't get to her. I picked up the pace, running harder, but just as I was about to catch up to her, she would somehow slip through my fingers, until she fell off the mountain all together. I woke up gasping and sweating and screaming her name. After that, I decided to try to work out these feelings with my fists. Besides, I needed something to do.

The gym is quiet. It's late for a weekend night and I'm guessing most people are home with their families or out with their friends. There's a couple people working the front desk and that's it. It's just me, the pounding of the music they have playing through the speakers, and the bag in front of me.

As I pound into it, ire and despair battle it out inside of me. I've replayed our time together so many times that through the cracks of remembrance another thought seeps through. Tatum's revelation from the night before finally resonates. I've been so caught up in her leaving, that I hadn't let myself think about anything else. But now that she's gone and there's nothing I can do about it, my thoughts turn to Jerry, and how he's been playing me all this time. It's no great surprise really. I had no idea that Tatum switched schools, no idea that she wasn't exactly where Jerry had told me she was all that time. I have no one to blame but myself. He would give me small updates on things, offer supposed evidence, and I would simply believe him. Talking about her or seeing the proof shoved in my face that she was gone and living her life without me was something I was unwilling to focus on too much – I couldn't. So I never delved deeper, never asked him to expand on any detail, never looked closely at any receipt he gave me. I just nodded my head and kept working toward wrapping up our deal. Always trying to become a stronger, faster, smarter fighter so I could end my tie to the man.

The more I think about it, how he's lied, taken advantage, manipulated and used me for his own benefit, plus the amount of money he's taken from me over the years, the more furious I become. My jabs come faster, harder, my breaths rapid. Sweat pours down my face and chest in rivers.

I'm so engrossed in my efforts that I don't hear anyone approach, until his voice is in my ear. "Where was this shit at the fight last night, you bastard? Maybe if you had put in this kind of effort, you wouldn't have gotten your ass kicked. Instead you looked like a pussy that could barely stand up and block a jab. The least you could have done was try to look worthy of being in the ring while you took a beating." He laughs and my whole body stiffens at the sound. My arms drop, I turn around slowly to face him, my breaths rapid before, now come in heaves. He keeps laughing, no idea that he's poking a bear.

"What are you looking at?" He slurs, clearly as drunk as always. He never changes. "Get back to work. Clearly you need some more training, so don't let me stop you."

"Shut up. Don't talk to me like that," I tell him.

"What was that?" He asks half turned away from me.

"I'm not your punching bag, so shut up," I state firmly.

"What did you say to me, boy?"

"I said, shut the fuck up." I practically yell this time, enunciating each word. From my periphery someone at the front desk looks our way.

"Where do you get off talking to me like that? Clearly I'm right, the bruises on your face are evidence enough. It's more training you need. Not only on your fighting, but now you're also forgetting who's in charge here."

This time, it's me that laughs, and Jerry's eyes bulge. I've never back talked him, not once in five years. I never wanted to do anything to jeopardize Tatum's situation, her scholarship, or her financial security. When I knew she should have graduated, it was my outstanding debt that called me to alignment with our agreement. So, I kept my mouth closed, and my head down, because what was the point? A deal was a deal. I may be lacking in several ways, but I've always prided myself on being a man of my word. In my mind, I was still doing what I agreed to do in order to put my girl through school, whether she had finished her studies or not. So instead, I counted down the days until our contract was up. He may have milked me for far more money than I owed, but the amount kept dwindling on the invoices so I just focused on that. But now... now I know that our deal has long since been over. And the way it feels to be free of him for the first time in five years? The feeling I felt when I finally confessed everything I've been holding in for so long? Well, it starts spreading through me again, and the feeling makes me laugh outright.

"What the hell is wrong with you?" Jerry asks confusion all over his face and I fucking love it.

"I'm done."

"Excuse me?"

"You heard me. I'm so done, with all of this. I'm not fighting another day for you as long as I live."

Suddenly, Jerry seems to have sobered up a bit. "I have a contract that says differently."

"You can take that contract and shove it up your ass, Jerry." I lean in close to his face, and smirk, "You see, you have nothing to hang over me anymore. *I know.*"

"Know...what? What the hell are you talking about?"

"I know that I paid you in full long ago and all this time, you've been milking me, taking advantage of me. My debt is paid. It's over. And so, I'm telling you, I'm done. You've used me for the last time."

"I will take your ass to court. I have a contract that says you will pay me back every dime I spent to send that bitch of yours to school."

"And I'm telling you again that you can take that contract and shove it up your ass because you know, as well as I do, that all it will take is one call to the Institute of Art to find out that Tatum left that school after two years, not four. I've been paying you for five long years. My payments to you have amounted to thousands upon thousands. I've long since paid you back. So go ahead, I *dare you* to try. Please – I beg you. Give me a reason to prove what you've done and then it will be *you* that has to pay *me* back. Go ahead and take me to court, see what happens."

He holds my stare for a moment before he does something I'm not expecting. I thought he'd rant, rave, deny, yell, scream, deal out more insults like usual, but instead he laughs. He laughs and laughs and laughs. Tears stream down his face, and he's bent over, hands on his knees. I should walk away, end this now, but instead I find myself staring at him in utter confusion and curiosity. I have no idea what's so funny. "Oh god, I can't catch my breath," he says while wiping at his face with the back of his hand. "You're right. The contract, which I never filed with the court or got notarized by the way, couldn't hold a candle in court. You never even looked at the copy you received did you? You're fucking stupid, so naïve, so stupid and were so butt hurt over a stupid whore, that I milked it for as long as I could. I sure as hell did get away with it for a long time. I thought for sure I'd still get a couple of more years yet."

I'm struck speechless, not sure at all what to say, so I voice the first thing that comes to me, "Why? Why did you do that?"

"Why not? I'll never forget the day that I overheard you talking in the gym locker room to Ryder. You were crying like a girl and going on like a damn idiot about your piece of ass. How sad you were that she wasn't being herself, and that she was never happy, that nothing you said or did was enough, that you were worried about her health. You were a sad sack of shit. Pathetic. The longer I listened, the more I knew that I had walked in on the perfect opportunity. I mean, my god, what good luck! Finally!"

"I'm not listening to anymore of this. I changed my mind, I don't care why."

"Too fucking bad, I'm not finished."

"Yes, you are." I tell him and I turn toward the entrance, ready to leave and get far away from him and this godforsaken place.

"NO!" Jerry screams and I ignore him. "No son of mine is going to walk away from me again. Get your ass back here." At that, I stop. My stomach drops to my feet and I'm sure I misheard. "That's right. You heard me. Son. Worst mistake I ever made was getting that bitch mother of yours pregnant. But it's okay, I got mine."

Turning slowly, I face him again, my mind turning so fast I'm not sure I can voice any one thought quite yet.

"Shocked, are you? You know I wasn't sure if maybe you knew. Part of me thought maybe that was the reason you stayed and dealt with my shit for so long. I thought maybe your mom had broken her word and ended up telling you after all, but I can see by the look on your face that she didn't. I guess maybe she was good for something, because let me tell you, she sure as hell wasn't worth the risk I took. And she was just as naïve as you. Guess it runs in the genes."

He and my mother. My mother and Jerry. I can't make sense of it. My head is spinning wicked fast and I swallow constantly because I'm confident I'm going to throw up.

"I sent your mother money. Every month, like clockwork. I told her I would help support you and watch out for you over the years if she would keep her damn mouth shut. I didn't want her running to my wife and making shit impossible with her or my father. She agreed, more concerned with taking care of you than any misguided feelings she thought she had for me, so I kept up my end of the deal. The day I heard you in the locker room, it was so perfect I couldn't even believe it. Making my son pay me back for all the money I had to spend on him over the years when he was younger? Sweet fucking justice."

My mom. He treated her like a piece of garbage. I should be angry with her for doing this, angry she never told me the truth, but somehow through the chaos in my mind, I'm able to understand. I know that being a single mom was hard for her. I remember her always trying to compensate for the fact that I didn't have a father to teach me to change a tire, hit or catch a ball, or even throw a punch when I developed a love for fighting. My mom did what she could and encouraged me to participate in activities, no matter how much they would cost, or the time they required. She was everything I needed. It was hard to miss something you never had to begin with anyway. So, I didn't. I went through a stage where I asked questions and wondered about my father, sure, but she wasn't willing to answer, so I finally quit asking.

Never, not once, would I ever have thought that this disgusting excuse for a human being in front of me could be my father. Looking into his eyes, I can't find a shred of decency. Not one fleck of humanity. The thought that I come from him... I can't even go there right now.

He starts to laugh again. I don't know if it's the look on my face that amuses him, or what, but before I think twice I have the front of his shirt in my left fist and my right one flies against his face. He falls and I go down with him. I feel deep satisfaction when I see blood in the corner of his mouth and I cock my fist back to hit him again. I want to beat the shit out of him. He has no heart, so there's only one way he can feel part of the pain he's caused me over the years, and that's physically. But something stops me. I'm not sure what. But looking into his face, I suddenly feel so fucking tired. Exhaustion weighs down on my shoulders and somehow I'm able to let go of him, and stand.

"That's it? That's all you've got?" he begins to taunt me, but I ignore him. I turn and with him screaming at me to get back there, I walk out of the gym. I calmly walk to my car, get inside, and after a minute, know exactly where I need to go.

It takes me no time at all to get there. I'm not even sure if anyone will be there, but I pray to god they are. Walking inside X-Treme Fitness Center, I stop in the doorway for a minute and look around. Some of the guys are fighting in the octagon and lifting weights and I immediately calm at seeing them. I want to tell all of them the truth; I feel like I owe that to them. They've all been worried, have all asked me together, or individually what's going on, but there's someone that deserves to talk to me alone first.

Heading towards Jax's office, I take several deep breaths. I hope he's inside yet dread it at the same time. As I approach I can see the door is open, and as I get a view of the interior. I see he's there, behind his desk, buried in paperwork. "I wasn't sure if you would still be here this late," I say by way of greeting.

"Cole," he says when his head pops up at my voice, "I'm surprised to see you here so late. On a Friday. This is unusual." I nod, swallowing hard, trying to decide where to begin. "I told Rowan I would be late tonight because I have some end of month paperwork to finish up, otherwise you're right, I'd be home by now."

"I'm sorry to interrupt, I can talk to you later," I tell him slightly backing out of the doorway while half hoping he will take me up on it but knowing he won't, because he's too kind.

"No, it's fine. What's going on? There's got to be a reason you're here this late. It's not the norm."

"I...there's something I have to tell you, but man, I have to be honest and tell you I'm not sure how. I'm still trying to process everything myself. I just...got in my car and found myself here."

"Okay. Is this about Tatum? Why she's here?"

"Yes. And no. I guess," I swallow and before I can try to put my thoughts into words, we're interrupted.

"Jax, you need to put in an order for some more-" Ryder begins but stops when he sees me sitting here. "Cole, what are you doing here?"

Their reactions to my presence makes me feel guilty that I haven't been here in a while. And when I have, it's never for long, not the last few months anyway. "I…I need to talk to Jax."

Ryder's brow lowers and he frowns. His arms cross over his chest and I can tell he's worried and there's no way in hell he's going to leave. "What's going on?"

I look at Jax and hesitate knowing what I have to tell him and feeling unsure how to proceed. So, I just blurt out, "I punched Jerry," which is not at all what I intend to say.

Ryder smiles and Jax looks concerned, and not for his dad. "What did he do?" Jax asks.

Rubbing my temples, I sigh, "Ryder?"

"Yeah?"

"Close the door. And you're going to want to sit down."

Ryder obeys without a word and with both of their eyes on me, I take a deep breath and begin, "Five years ago, Jerry approached me with a deal." I tell them everything. Remind them how bad Tatum was after we lost the baby, about the talk Ryder and I had in the locker room, which he remembers. Tell them how Jerry overheard and how he approached me, that I agreed, the stipulations, how I broke Tatum, and myself in the process. I tell them why I've been putting up with Jerry's shit. That I felt like it was the only way to take care of Tatum. That I've had no say in anything fighting related, that I signed a contract. Ryder begins pacing the floor, unable to stay seated. Jax's face never changes, he sits still and watches me closely taking it all in.

"I can't believe you've been dealing with this bastard all this time and you've never said a word," Jax says. "I could have told you that half of everything he says and does is a lie. Hell, I could have helped you through this. If you had only said something."

"I couldn't. I felt like it was the right thing at the time. And when things got bad, there was no way I could bring myself to ask for

help. Admitting that I fucked up? Not exactly an easy thing to do."
I hesitate, "But, there's something else…something Jerry said, and
while I know he's a cheat and a liar, I don't think he was lying about
this."

"Oh god, I can't wait to hear this," Ryder says.

"He…" I look at Jax, really look at him, and for the first time, I can
find some similarities. The shape of our eyes is similar, our chins. It's
funny that given what I know about Jerry, I'm not questioning this.
"He's my father," I practically whisper, the prospect feeling strange
and the words foreign on my tongue.

"He's what?" Jax says. "What do you mean?"

"He told me that I'm his son," I tell him, and then explain
everything that happened when I tried to walk away from Jerry
before he was done spewing his hate on me.

When I finish, Ryder looks between the two of us in utter shock
and Jax has his hands folded on his desk and hasn't looked away
from them since I started speaking. "Jax, I'm sorry. I didn't know."

Jax stands up and moves to my side of the desk and sits in the
chair next to me. "Why are you apologizing?"

"Because, I feel like this is all my fault, but I didn't know.
Honestly, I had no idea."

"It doesn't matter even if you did. I fucking hate the fact that
you've been dealing with this shit on your own for so long. We've
asked you over and over again why you were so loyal to Jerry, and
now I get why you never said. I'd like to say that I'm surprised, but
I'd be lying, because I'm not. Jerry was never faithful to my mom.
I knew, my grandfather knew, and unfortunately my mother knew
how he was. It's not surprising to me that he fathered another child
out of his infidelity."

I remain quiet, confused with the mixture of feelings I have. On
one hand, I'm angry as hell. I'm angry at Jerry, angry at my mom,
devastated over Tatum, elated over the fact Jax is my half-brother,

yet also dismayed. I struggle to find words but Jax again beats me to the punch, "Cole, you've always been my brother. We're all brothers," he says gesturing to Ryder and I know he means all the other guys too. "The only difference is that we know with us, that we're brothers by blood too."

And then, he reaches over and hugs me, and hell if it isn't exactly what I need. I blink back the burning sensation in my eyes and as we pull away and I nod my head at him and smile for the first time in what feels like forever, Ryder says, "Aw, well wasn't that adorable?"

We all laugh and Jax mutters, "Shut the fuck up," and while there are so many things that I don't know right now, one thing I do know is that I'm lucky as hell to have these guys in my life. I know I can get through anything, maybe even the loss of Tatum again, with their help. I'll just never admit that to them. I'd never live it down.

CHAPTER FOURTEEN

Tatum

Someone should explain to me why we need men. I mean, other than procreation. Aside, from that, why? I mean, when I'm ready to get pregnant again, there's something to be said for being able to walk into a sperm bank, pick out a daddy from a binder full of attributes and descriptions and simply getting the job done. I could be a single mom, I mean, sure it would be hard, but I could do it. I don't need a man. Maybe I can find myself a best friend and we can raise a child together as platonic life partners. I don't need sex, right? There are toys for that anyway. I roll my eyes at my absurdity, I'm being ridiculous and I know it. It's just this and many other crazy thoughts have been running through my mind ever since Cole's confession.

Perhaps I'm trying to keep myself from delving too deep into analyzing everything Cole said. My mind prefers to fluctuate all over the place – from one extreme to the other. I'm angry one second – ready to do away with the whole male race – and then the next, I'm sad for the circumstances we've found ourselves in over the last five years and so crazy in love with him that I can't see straight.

We've missed so much time together. When I think about every second we've spent apart it makes me hurt. When I consider everything Cole's gone through in order to take care of me, I'm both furious and touched. I want to both slap him for it, and praise him. He gave up everything. Me, yes, but more. He sacrificed his dreams, goals, college, some important decisions, and likely lots more I'll never know about — all to protect me, to care for me. And while the last couple years or so have certainly been more about him protecting himself and his dignity, it doesn't change that the foundation derived from his love for me.

That's why when I got up and drove to the airport, I found myself unable to go through with leaving. I couldn't get on the plane. I stood there, driver's license in hand, ready to go to the counter in order to check my bags and obtain my ticket, but found myself unable to move. It was busy and people moved around me in constant activity, while I stood there, in the middle of it all seeing nothing but Cole's face before me. I couldn't leave. Not yet.

I turned around, made my way to the rental car area, rented another car and left. I had no destination in mind. I drove aimlessly for a long time. Somehow I found myself sitting next to Hope's grave again. Tracing the letters of her name I poured my heart out to her. I told her that I love her dad. That while I tried to get on with my life and even though I did so in Chicago, that I couldn't even count the times that thoughts of him entered my mind because it was so often. People or things could easily trigger memories. I would push them away, eager to convince myself I was moving on. Therapy helped me heal and deal with the loss of Hope, but it wasn't an eraser of feelings. Just like it didn't have the power to make me eradicate my sadness wrought from the loss of my daughter, it also didn't have the power to make me stop loving or missing Cole. And I never did. I tried to cover it, bury it, move on from it, ignore it, pretend it wasn't there, chalked it up to my imagination, a mistake, anything and everything to simply get it to go away. And it did for a while. I buried it quite deeply. Through moving on with my life. Going through the motions. Being with Blaine. But isn't it funny how our true feelings have a way of manifesting anyway? All anyone has to do is look at my art over the years to see that. Cole has always been a constant presence. Always.

Telling Hope I loved her and thanking her for listening to her crazy mom, I found myself at a loss of where to go or what to do.

Until I find myself staring at my old dormitory – unknowingly I took myself back to the start. Where I first met Cole. The memory of shutting the door in his face makes me smile. I find myself walking the campus, reminiscing about places we sat and studied together, a huge landscape rock we used to meet at between classes before we would leave and go have lunch together.

Swinging by Porky's BBQ I eat a sandwich, sit in our typical spot and remember all the times we sat there studying together that first year. All the random conversations we had, dreams we made together and laughs we shared. There was so much love between us. People say that young people don't really know the meaning of love, but I disagree. I think when you find the person you're supposed to be with that it isn't about finding love – love finds you. At least that how it felt for us. Our souls merged and from that moment on, it took a miracle or I guess in our case a tragedy to break us apart. But the funny thing is, the foundation, the roots of our love, are still entwined. All this time they've continued to twist together, grow, become deeper, just waiting for the moment, the time when they could branch out and grow once more.

I'm so caught up in my thoughts that when the thought occurs to me to show up at my next location, I guess I didn't really think it through that hard. I spent so much time with Cole here, that it makes sense. It was our home away from home. A place we could be alone sometimes, and one we just liked hanging out at when we could. I asked him about his mom, careful with my questions because she'd always been an emotional topic for me. When I left Cole, I left her too. Darla was always like my second mother. When not working, which seemed to be so often, she lavished on us with her excellent cooking. She was always extremely loving, caring, and she took an interest in our lives and treated me like her own.

Cole said she's still in Arizona, but I have no idea if she still lives here. But as I stare at the small stucco house, and take in some similarities and differences, I close my eyes and see it as it was five years ago. I remember the beloved pots of flowers she would keep out front, the small bench that she would sit on at times while she'd watch the neighborhood kids play in the evening while she drank sweet tea and chatted with her neighbors. She always wore an apron and her dark hair was always pulled on top of her head. Her smiles were often, the food she made comforting, and her hugs felt like coming home.

"Tatum?" My eyes snap open, and I'm so caught up in the memory of her that I hardly know what to think when my vision manifests to life in front of me. Blinking rapidly, I focus and realize she's standing in front of me. "Ms. Russell?"

"Tatum! Well I thought that was you. I was doing dishes and happened to look out the window and saw you standing here. I almost didn't believe my eyes. What are you doing here?" I open my mouth to tell her but nothing emerges, as I'm not even sure where to begin or what to say. "Never mind that. Get yourself over here and give me a hug."

With a big smile, I run across the yard and do just that. When she wraps me up in her arms, the tears come immediately - fast and furious. What is it about the love of a mother that brings forth emotions so intently? A friend can ask you if you're doing okay when you're not, you smile and nod and tell them you're fine. But then when your mother asks, you begin to bawl your eyes out, not able to smile and pretend. It's like they have a way of looking at you with eyes that tell you they know the truth so there's no point in lying, and so the emotions break free. There's so much love in their comforting arms. I'm sure it has everything to do with our parent's being our safe place – if we're lucky enough to have that kind of relationship with them.

"Oh sugar, it will be okay," she tells me rubbing my back, while steering me into her home. As soon as I walk in the front door, the smell, the familiar setting, it all makes me cry harder. We sit on the couch and she continues to rub my back and murmur to me until I calm myself.

"I'm so, so, sorry Ms. Russell."

"Honey, I've told you plenty of times to call me Darla. Stop with this Ms. Russell business," she tells me as if she just scolded me yesterday, not years ago. "Now what's going on? I have a feeling this has to do with that boy of mine."

"That boy of yours is wonderful. And I've missed him so much," I tell her honestly.

"Oh honey, why does saying that make you cry?"

"Because I may have screwed up, because I've been confused, because I have been so selfish that if I were him, I wouldn't want to take me back. And, because I'm scared."

She smiles softly and pushes a stray strand of hair behind my ear, "Oh, is that all?" She laughs softly and it makes me laugh too. "He's never been the same since you left you know," she tells me. "I'm not going to intrude, it's not my business, and if there's anything to tell, I should hear it from him," she kindly, yet firmly instructs and I nod, "But, I will tell you that my boy, he loved you with everything he had, and I know that you've never been far from his mind, even after all this time. If I can help in any way, I'm here. If you just need to sit here, that's fine too. Whatever you need."

"I just…" I sigh and swipe at my eyes, "Cole did something for me, but didn't tell me about it. He should tell you the details, but your son, is a great man. What he did… he made a decision to take care of me in a way that was a sacrifice to himself. I'm angry that he made that choice without consulting me, and at the time, I thought he did it because he didn't want to be with me anymore. Because, I failed him when I lost our baby. I just found out the truth about what happened, and well, I'm feeling a lot of things that I'm trying to define to be honest."

She follows me the best she can, confusion on her face clear, but she pats my leg, "Let me repeat, if there is one thing I know, it's that my boy loves you and has never stopped. After the loss of little Hope," she smiles sadly, "he was sad and devastated. But after the loss of you, when you left...he was broken." Her eyes reflect her pain at the words and it feels like a stab of guilt in my heart. She must see something on my face because she pats my leg again, "I'm not telling you that to hurt you, I'm telling you because I want you to know that he told me a little of the same thing that you did. That he had to do something to help you and unfortunately that meant that you needed to leave. To go to art school, but honey, I know whatever it was, it wasn't easy for him, and since then, my boy... he's just not been the same. Sure, he tries to fool me, he smiles and goes through the motions, but a mother knows her son. And I know that a part of him has been lost without you."

Tears fall in streams down my face, "I've been lost without him too. We spent some time together this week, I've been in town for an art show, and we happened to see each other. It felt like fate running into him. I didn't realize how lost I've been until being with him again this week made me start to feel whole again in a way I didn't even realize I could be. Not since Hope, anyway. I started to feel like myself again."

"Well then honey, call me crazy, but I don't understand the problem. Why are you here and not with my boy?"

"A couple reasons. First, I needed to gather my thoughts after learning a few things. My initial reaction was to push him away. I needed space to process," she nods as if this makes complete sense, "and also because I'm afraid," I whisper.

"Afraid? What do you mean?"

"I'm afraid to let myself love him again." Part of me can't believe I've admitted this to his mother, yet at the same time, I know being here is exactly where I'm supposed to be. "What happens if we can't work it out after all? What happens if I ruined it already because I didn't immediately see his side of things? What if…" and I pause because this is the big one, the feeling buried so deep down that digging it up is physically painful. I practically choke on the words. "What if we find our way back to each other only to end up in exactly the same place once more? What if we try again to have a baby some day and I…and I…"

She places her hand on the side of my face and looks deep into my eyes, "Then you will deal with it. Surely you know by now that what happened is not your fault."

"Yes, and no. I have good days and bad days."

"Fair enough, but take it from me, we each have our share of good and bad things. Some of which we have no control over. And you know, good and bad isn't all that clear sometimes. Some things that seem bad at the time, actually have good outcomes in the bigger picture of life. Yes, I believe that there's a bigger picture. We don't know now what that is, but one day, when we meet our maker, we'll find out. We'll see it all and know why things happened, what the bigger meaning is, why our pain was necessary and mattered. I know that the loss of that baby girl wasn't for nothing. I have faith in that. Now believe me or not, that's okay, to each our own, but what I do know is that whatever this is you are speaking of, whatever it is that drew you apart, was horrible. You both made decisions afterwards that it sounds like you wish were different and that you regret."

"Yes," I nod. I got all over Cole for not calling, not having contact, not telling me the truth, but the fact is that I never tried to reach out to him again either. I thought about it, hell I thought about it a lot, but I still didn't do it. I let my stubborn pride keep me from being the first one to reach out. I'm not blameless.

"Well the thing about making mistakes, is that hopefully we learn from them. We don't always get it right the first time every time, you know. Don't be so hard on yourself. Because the great thing is, the both of you will learn from this. Your love will get you through."

"Will it, Darla?" I ask softly, "Because sometimes, love isn't enough."

"No. Love is always enough, if you build it correctly."

"I don't know what you mean."

"Look at it this way, when you build a home, you don't just lay the foundation, even a good one, and call it complete, right? You build walls, a roof. You use padding, cement, shingles, wood and nails. You use other things to make that house as sturdy as possible so that it can endure anything. Love is no different. Love is always enough if you build it strong enough. You wrap it in trust, layer it with understanding, pad it with loyalty, nail in fun, memories, honor, and compromise. Before you know it this pliable, vulnerable thing becomes unyielding and indestructible - a complete structure. That, my dear, is why love is always enough, and that is also why you and Cole will be just fine."

And somehow I believe her. Because, while her hugs have always felt like home, her words have always seemed like promises, and I know the words she speaks now are exactly that.

CHAPTER FIFTEEN

Cole

When I wake in the morning, I groan loudly, my head aching from overindulgence the night before. After telling Ryder and Jax everything, not only about Jerry, but about Tatum too, Ryder's brilliant suggestion was that we partake in some drinking. He said it would help dull my pain or some shit. I honestly didn't care about his reasoning. I was all too eager to take him up on it. Especially when Jax pulled a bottle of whiskey out of his desk. He had some plastic cups and we took turns filling up our glasses while we traded memories and shots at Jerry until the wee hours of the morning.

Ryder and I stumbled down the street back home, and I was thankful once again for the fact that we live within walking distance. All too happy to collapse into bed the second I got home, I don't remember lying there long before I was out immediately. One good thing came from drinking, and that's the fact that I slept like a log. Given the day I had yesterday, it's really no surprise – I was exhausted – but I'm thankful there wasn't a dream to be had. The reprieve from the last twenty-four hours was very much needed.

Getting up, I start the coffee pot, and look for pain reliever while I wait for it to brew. I'm dreading a conversation I need to have today. I contemplate putting it off, but I know that the sooner I get it over with the better. It would only drive me crazy until then, and I've had enough crazy to last me a lifetime.

Taking my coffee with me into the shower, it isn't long before the combination of caffeine and warm water has me feeling better. I take my time, lingering, knowing that all I'm doing is stalling. With a sigh, I turn off the water and dress quickly.

As soon as I step out of my apartment a half hour later, I've barely got my door locked before Ryder's door swings open down the hall and he peeks his head out. If I didn't know better, I'd swear he'd been listening for me. He looks as hung over as I'm sure I did when I woke up and I smile widely, "Wishing we had quit while we were ahead?"

"Nah, where's the fun in that? Where you headed? Need company?"

Now I'm thinking that maybe it isn't so crazy thinking he was listening for me after all. "No, I'm good. I have an errand to run. Alone."

"You sure? It will only take me a few minutes to throw some clothes on," he says while his hand disappears to scratch, I don't even want to know what.

"Dude, are you naked?" He just smiles and I roll my eyes, "I'm fine. Really. Thanks though, man."

"This doesn't have to do with Jerry, right? You aren't going to see him?"

"No," I state firmly. "I have no desire to see Jerry. Maybe not ever again."

"Okay. Good. But call me if you need me, alright?"

"Alright fine. But can I go now, before we start growing girl parts?"

"Fuck you," he says, but not before he laughs. When he turns around, his bare ass is there in all it's glory for anyone to see and I shake my head. Just before he disappears behind his door, he turns back and winks at me over his shoulder. I can't help but laugh, then groan a little at the ache that doing so creates in my head.

Getting into my car, I turn my mind to the conversation ahead, not sure how I'm going to approach what I'm about to do. Truth is, I'm still trying to make sense out of a mixture of emotions. At the forefront is still the pain over Tatum's leaving. I wish she had given me a chance to talk to her more, but maybe I need to have some patience. I'm hopeful she needs a few days and then will somehow contact me. She knows the name of Jax's gym; it would be easy for her to find me. And if she doesn't, well, as far as I'm concerned things between us aren't over. I'll find her if it's the last thing I do.

Putting that aside for now, my thoughts move to Jax's suggestion last night. He thinks I should threaten to sue Jerry. Tell him he either pays me back the money he defrauded from me, or I'll let a judge decide our fate, which would potentially alarm Jerry because I could be awarded damages. Jax said I don't really have to do any of it, but he has some attorney contacts through the gym that can help us scare Jerry, if nothing else. The attorney would draw up some papers and make threatening demands likely through a lot of legal jargon and veiled threats. He doesn't think I should let him get away with what he's done.

I'm honestly not sure what I want to do yet. Does scaring the fuck out of him sound appealing? Hell yes. Does making him have to pay for what he's done seem like the perfect payback? Of course it does. But, I hesitate because a part of me, and I think a bigger part, is just so damn happy to be rid of him, the thought of drawing any of this out longer makes me want to puke.

He finally has nothing on me anymore. No hold over me, nothing he can threaten me with, nothing he can do about it either. He can sure as hell try, but he won't. Jax agrees. Jerry already admitted the contract was crap. While I'll be fine to never have contact with the man again, there is a small piece of me that wants justice. That feels like he should pay for what he did to me. To my mom. Hell, even to Jax. But, I really do think I'll be happy to have him in my rearview mirror, nothing more. I do know that whatever I decide, Jax is behind me one hundred percent.

This brother thing is strange, but he's the best thing to come out of this by far. We'll try to maneuver our way through this the best way we know how, but really what he said last night is true – he's already my brother. In my mind, all the guys are my brothers, we've all been together so long. I'm just going to take it one day at a time, I don't think there's any other way to deal with it all. Jax has promised to do whatever he can to keep Jerry away from me. He apologized so many times it's stupid. It isn't his fault, and I don't blame him at all. I'm the one that made the deal with Jerry, I'm the one that never said a word about any of it to anyone. The choice was all mine. I told him until I was blue in the face that he's not responsible for the actions of his, uh our, father, but I don't think he agrees.

With a deep breath, I try to move my thoughts to the task before me. I try to play out all the various avenues this could go in my mind, but I simply don't know what to expect. When I pull into the driveway of my mom's house, I walk slowly to the front door, dread filling my belly with each step. I consider turning around about a million times, but instead swallow down the sick feeling rising in my throat and keep walking. Knocking on the door a few times, I wait for a few moments, but when she doesn't answer, I walk inside, knowing her tendency to have the TV or music loud hinders her ability to hear the door. She must not be at the kitchen window, or she would have seen me walk up. When I step inside, I immediately smell bacon and coffee and it makes my stomach rumble. When I reach the kitchen, I find her at the stove, and lean against the doorway to watch her move around the kitchen. I love my mother, but how do I forgive her for being dishonest with me for so many years?

She's never been to a fight of mine. Not once. She hates it. Hates the fact I fight, has asked me to quit a million times. We've never agreed on the subject, have argued about it non-stop at times, so finally, I quit talking to her about it. She'd ask how things were going out of courtesy, and I'd tell her whatever I thought she wanted to hear. It was easier that way. As supportive as she is of me, she can't watch someone 'hit her boy for sport'. I get it – mostly- so we don't discuss it in depth anymore. Does that mean I've never once mentioned all this time that my trainer's name is Jerry? That she didn't know that he's been part of my life all along? I have a hard time wrapping my mind around any of it.

It takes her a moment to notice my presence and when she does, she jumps slightly and I frown when initially she doesn't seem too happy to see me. "Mom?"

"Hello," she walks to me and gives me a quick kiss on the cheek frowning and sighing at all the bruises on my face. "You broke your nose again?" I just shrug and she shakes her head. "I had a feeling you'd be coming around today."

That makes me suspicious. Could she have heard something? "You did? Why?"

"Just a feeling," she says without saying more.

"Do you have time to talk this morning? I have something I'd like to discuss with you."

"Well, sure honey, we can talk, but now may not be the best time."

"Why not?"

"Well-" she hedges.

I lose my patience, unable to keep it to myself anymore, "Mom, I know that Jerry Stone is my father."

The spatula that she's holding falls to the floor and she spins around to look at me. Her eyes instantly flood with tears and I'm not sure when the last time is that I've seen her emotional. "How? When? Are you...oh god," she sits down at the table and stares off into space. I take a seat at the table and wait for her to come back from wherever her mind has taken her. When she looks at me again, she says, "I promise I will explain."

"I think I already know some of it. He blackmailed you. He told you that he wouldn't help take care of me financially if you told me or anyone else about my parentage. And you agreed."

"I did. And I won't apologize for that," she states sternly.

"I didn't ask you to."

"I felt like a whore taking his money," she whispers and I flinch. "I felt like he was paying me off, but I was willing to swallow my pride over that feeling because all that mattered was being able to take care of you. So, I took his money if it meant that I was able to spend more time with you and less time at work, and if it meant it could help me provide for you in a way I wouldn't have been able to do otherwise. It was clear that he wasn't the man I thought he was, and the absence of him in your life wasn't something that I regretted one bit. I won't apologize for it, Cole. I've long since made peace with it all."

"Well isn't that great for you, mom. I, on the other hand, am just now finding out that my dead beat father is the man that I made a deal with in order to send Tatum to school and who's been blackmailing me for the last five years!"

"What? What are you talking about?"

And so I tell her. Everything. I don't leave a detail out. She knows how hard things were after Hope died, but I don't spare any details. I share my raw devastation at Tatum's leaving, how I lied to her face to get her to go, I tell her about the five long years of working to pay Jerry back, and his treatment of me in the process. I confess to her how I lost part of myself when Tatum left, and that he continued to chip away at me little by little over the years until what was left was someone I hardly recognized anymore. I tell her about running into Tatum, how I feel, my run in with Jerry, how he planned all of this. I spare no details, and she hardly speaks at all, only asking a clarifying question here and there, and we're only interrupted once by the burning smell of the bacon left in the frying pan. She pops out of her seat, puts the pan in the sink and gets right back to our conversation. She watches me intently, now and then a tear rolls down her cheek. Regret and sorrow on her face.

"Oh, Cole. I didn't know. Honest I didn't. I'd heard you mention your trainer here and there but it never occurred to me it was him. And after a while, when the money stopped coming and you were doing fine and more than capable of taking care of yourself, I let it go. Other than the questions you asked when you were younger, you never seemed interested in knowing more."

"I believe your exact words were something along the lines of, 'he's an asshole that wants nothing to do with what's likely the best thing he's ever done in his life. We don't need him.' I had no need for questions after that."

"No, I don't suppose you would," and she smiles and giggles which makes me chuckle too.

"I don't think it makes a whole lot of sense for me to be angry at you for not telling me about this, given I've lived the last several years of my life keeping secrets from everyone too. That would be hypocritical of me."

"You have every right to be upset with me, and I promise in time we will get through this, okay? If you are mad, let yourself be. If you have questions, ask them. I'm sorry, Cole. I shouldn't have been so selfish. I confess it was just fine with me that you never asked before how I could be with a man like that. The less you knew was more than fine with me. So, I let it go. I'm sorry."

"You don't have to apologize."

"I do, and I am. And I will for a while. Just placate your mother, okay?"

"Okay," I try to smile but don't quite manage.

"What is it?" she asks.

"It's nothing," I tell her and then change my mind. Tired of never really saying what I think. Tired of this person I've become, "Actually, it's something. I lost her again, mom. Tatum. And god it fucking hurts."

"Don't cuss in my kitchen."

"Sorry."

"I have a feeling that you and Tatum will be just fine."

"How can you say that?" I ask her.

"Your mom tends to be pretty smart about these kinds of things," a voice says from the kitchen doorway and I stand and spin around so fast the kitchen chair falls to the floor.

"Tatum." She's here. Standing in my mom's kitchen of all places. I'm seeing things. I have to be.

"Hi, Cole," she smiles shyly and my mom walks over to her and rubs her upper arm. The familiarity and the look that passes between them makes my heart clench.

"Good morning, dear. Did you sleep well?"

Tatum nods, "Yes, thank you."

"Sleep well?" I ask surprised. "You slept here?"

"Yes. Your mom let me stay in your old room."

"But, I thought…how are you…you didn't leave yesterday?"

She shakes her head, "How could I?" she asks and I'm torn between wanting to take her into my arms and never let her go, and demanding she explain herself right the hell now. "Can we…um… do you have time to talk?"

I nod, and my mom looks between us, and smiles. "Help yourself to whatever you want. I need to run to the grocery store to pick up a few things." She kisses me on the cheek, and Tatum too, then whispers in her ear. Tatum nods, and then she disappears and a moment later, we hear the front door close.

Tatum and I are alone, and I find that I'm not sure what to say. I open my mouth to say something, anything, but before I can, she holds up a hand in a silent request for me to remain quiet, "I have a few things I'd like to say."

"Okay," I reply, my throat feeling dry and scratchy.

"And, I want you to stay quiet until I'm finished. Can you do that?"

"Okay," I tell her again.

"Cole, when you told me about the deal you made with Jerry, and why everything happened between us the way it did my head, god, my head was spinning. At the forefront of my mind was that you made a decision for both of us. That while you claimed it was for me, that really it was all about you finding a way out of the mess that had become our lives."

I clench my teeth together, wanting to say something, but knowing I promised her I wouldn't.

"I was angry, hurt, and confused. Part of me also felt dismayed because you fooled me. I thought that I got into that school on my own merits, my talent, and so it hurt to find out it was really because a man like Jerry pulled strings to get me in. I felt like my choice was taken away. I felt I had nowhere else to go. My parents were all set to move as soon as my sister graduated high school, moving back with them wasn't an option. My life, it was supposed to be with you. Since you didn't want me anymore, taking that scholarship was the only option for me. And so, as you know, I did. I left. I moved on. Or at least I tried."

She begins picking her nails, and I'm not even sure she's aware of it. She worries her bottom lip between her teeth at times, and all I can think is that she's so fucking adorable it kills me. At times she stops and looks at me in the eyes, but it seems to be easier for her if she doesn't look at me too often.

"I buried myself in my school, my work. I sought out a therapist, as you know, and got help dealing with Hope's loss, and also...the loss of you." Her voice breaks a little and it makes my stomach clench. "Every day it became easier. I managed to bury my feelings, my past. But the funny thing is, even when I thought I had moved on, my subconscious was telling me through my art that I had done anything but. You've seen them. The paintings. Even when I didn't realize it, you were always there. With me. On my mind. In my heart. Always." She turns and looks at me, a tear escapes her eye and falls down her cheek and I want to step toward her and wipe it away, but I wait.

"Cole, you apologized to me. You bared your heart, your soul, told me the truth about everything, and I still…I still…" She stops and more tears fall down her face. I take a step toward her, but she shakes her head, "No. Please. I'm not finished. Cole, I'm the one that needs to beg you for forgiveness."

"What? No. Why would you say that?"

"Because, I never once stopped to think about you in all of this. When we lost Hope, I couldn't, god, I couldn't *bear* it. Living without her hurt. Trying to remember to do day-to-day activities was hard. I was lost in an abyss of darkness, despair, denial at times, and guilt. So. Much. Guilt. It was suffocating at times. But the thing is, if I had just taken one moment to stop and look around me, I wouldn't have had to bear any of it alone. You were there, right there, every step of the way. What was going on in my mind was awful, yes, but never once did I ever stop to think about you. I never stopped to consider how you were feeling, how you were coping with the loss, what you were thinking. I was so caught up in myself and my own grief, that I never stopped to consider yours. And I'm sorry. God, Cole, I am so fucking sorry."

"Tatum," I take another step, but she backs up, so I stop again, but I feel myself getting annoyed. I just want to touch her. Hold her. Wipe the tears from her face.

"When I agreed to come out here for a showing, I was hesitant at first. I knew it was the week of Hope's birth and I wasn't sure I could handle being here. Then I decided that it was actually the perfect place to be. I never expected I'd see you while I was here. I had no plans on trying to reach out, while my anger had long since subsided, my stubbornness was still fully intact," she smiles a little and I laugh knowing full well how stubborn of a woman she can be.

"I'm glad that I ended up running into you this week. If nothing else, I will always be grateful for the time we spent together. It's healed something inside of me that I assumed in my ignorance was long gone. It was hard at first, but I found that the more time I spent with you, the more of myself I found once again. But what I've also realized is that I am still totally, irrevocably and undeniably in love with you."

I don't think I could move if I wanted to now. Her words have frozen me to the spot. Her eyes search my face, looking for my response, but I'm incapable of giving her one. Her confession not at all what I expected. That is, until she gets down on her knees.

"I'm begging you. I will beg you every day for the rest of my life if I have to, to please forgive me. Please forgive me for being so selfish. Please forgive me for being so stubborn. I blame you for not having contact with me in all this time, while I was just as able to pick up a phone if I wanted to. I'm tired of living half a life. I'm tired of being without you. I know you still have feelings for me too, and I'm asking you for the chance to see if we can make this work. I've realized this week that what I've been missing all this time, the reason I still feel broken, is because you're carrying the missing pieces of me."

I'm on my knees and in front of her in seconds. I have her face in my hands and I'm kissing the hell out of her. I try to convey everything I'm feeling, everything I'm thinking in a kiss. But I know that she needs to hear the words too.

But first, I find a piece of me in her too, my sense of humor. "Can I talk now?" I ask her with a smile and she nods.

"Tatum, you don't owe me an apology," she starts to protest but I shut her up with a kiss and she smiles. "I think it's safe to say that we both handled each other poorly back then. But, I say we give each other a break. We suffered a horrible loss and we didn't know how to deal with it, I don't know that many people in the same situation would. Tatum, I have never stopped loving you. You've never been far from my mind, my heart. I want you forever. Always."

"I'll move back here, Cole. I want to. I want to be with you here."

"I planned on giving you a couple days and if I hadn't heard from you I was going to come after you. I was going to find you and tell you the same thing. That I love you. Want to be with you and I will go to Chicago if that's what you want."

"No. I want to be here. This is home. You're my home."

I kiss her again and then pull her up. "Let's get out of here. I need to be with you. And call me crazy, but I'm not really wanting to have my mom walk in and create an awkward moment for her and us."

She laughs and after scribbling a quick note to my mom, we grab her luggage from my room, as well as a couple things she left in her rental car. Not wanting to deal with her car right now, we decide to leave it here to take care of later. We laugh and kiss all the way up the stairs to my apartment. As I reach for the keys in my pocket, her hands travel up my back, down my ass, and wrap around my waist. Turning to face her, I take her mouth with mine. She moans and I turn and place her back against the door while I continue to kiss her, my tongue exploring her mouth, darting in and out and teasing her.

Her hands move to my waist and she undoes my jeans, and surprises me by shoving her hands down the back of my pants, making me laugh. Just as I turn the lock, a door across the hall opens and I know without looking it's Ryder. "Well, well, well, lookie what we have here," he says, and I can hear the amusement in his voice.

"Are you naked again? Should I cover Tatum's eyes?" I ask and smile when her eyes widen. I whisper, "He spoke to me as I left earlier and mooned me when he walked back into his apartment," I tell her with a roll of my eyes.

"Secrets don't make friends," Ryder says and I finally glance at him over my shoulder. "What are you? Twelve?"

Tatum giggles and the sound makes my heart soar in my chest. "I've gotta go, Ryder. Talk later, yeah?"

"Yeah, okay."

"Oh, Ryder?" Tatum says.

"Yes, Tatum, love?" he says and I narrow my eyes at him which makes him smile gleefully.

Before I can say a word, Tatum surprises me by pulling my pants down, and I feel air brush across my bare ass as I'm suddenly mooning Ryder. Tatum squeals out a laugh, Ryder makes some comment about never needing to see that again, and I...well I bust up laughing, and it feels so good.

Turning the lock, we stumble inside my apartment, and I pull her back to my room. "I was thinking this time we could make it to the bed, instead of the floor."

"Well if you insist," she says with a smile and then pushes away from me. She maintains eye contact while she begins to take off her clothes and I'm so caught up in watching her reveal her flesh inch by inch that when she raises an eyebrow, it takes me a minute to realize she's wanting me to take my clothes off too. "Yes, ma'am," I tell her not needing her to voice her command.

When we are naked, we each devour the other with our eyes. I reach out a finger and trace her cheekbone, run it down her neck to her clavicle. I run it down her chest, circle her breast and then move down her stomach and to the curly patch of hair below until I touch her intimately and stroke. Her head falls back on her shoulders and she moans. Stepping toward her I kiss her neck, nibble along her jaw line, and move up to her ear lobe and nibble remembering how she used to love it. I'm rewarded with another moan from her.

Taking her by the waist, I pick her up and take her to my bed. Starting at her mouth, I kiss my way down her body, then push her legs open so I can pleasure her with my mouth. Her hands grip my head, her moans and whispers of encouragement spurn me on. When she finds release, I look at her and smile, and she pushes against my chest, "Lie on your back," she instructs and I quickly obey.

Rising over me, she kisses down my body and intends to return the favor, but I stop her. "No. I want to be inside of you. Now. I need you."

She nods and rises above me. Hands balanced on my chest, eyes locked on mine, we become one. As she moves over me, my heart expands in my chest, more and more until it feels like it's going to explode. "I love you," I tell her. My mind, my body, my heart consumed with her.

"I love you too, Cole. Always and forever."

"Forever," I repeat, then bring her mouth down to mine.

CHAPTER SIXTEEN

Tatum

I'm not sure what wakes me. But when I look at the clock on the bedside table in Cole's room, I see that it's early yet, only seven in the morning. We barely slept last night. Too consumed with one another to allow ourselves to sleep for long. We were rediscovering one another, making up for lost time I suppose.

Slipping out of bed, I pause and take a look around the room. My paintings cover every single wall; now, looking at them makes me smile. They make me feel happiness and contentment. There's something comforting knowing that I've always been here with him.

My fingers itch to paint. I told Cole last night that I want to go to the store today and get some canvases, easels and paints. I'm feeling inspired and the need to create is making me feel twitchy. I want to paint his likeness – his face, his hands. I want to paint the look in his eyes when he captures a glance of me from across the room, and the smile upon his face when he's returning one I send his way.

Quickly ducking into the kitchen, I open the refrigerator to see if he has the fixings for breakfast. I'd like to surprise him with breakfast in bed maybe, or hell, just breakfast, who the hell cares where. I just want to spend the morning with him, every morning with him. Happy, and a bit surprised, I spot eggs, bacon and orange juice. I can toast the bread on the counter – and whip a simple, easy meal. I decide to duck into the bathroom to freshen up first.

Stripping off Cole's t-shirt I stole from his drawer, I wait for the shower water to warm up and ease under the water to rinse off. I take my time, enjoying the scent of Cole's shampoo and soap. I smell each one, and rub them all over my body and wash my hair. As I run the soap over my body I smile at the love bites I find all over, and my mind goes back to the night before. The way his body felt on mine, taking time to rediscover parts of him I always loved, and muscles that are more defined, and tattoos that have appeared since the last time I was able to take the time to explore him.

Turning off the water, eager to get back to Cole, I quickly towel dry off and grab my makeup case. Cole went to his car and brought all my things inside for me and I'm happy he did so, when I reach for my toothbrush. After I finish, I'm about to open the door and turn off the light, when I happen to catch my reflection in the mirror.

Moving closer, my eyes trace the lines of my face like always, and I look into my own eyes. I try to see it. Like I always do. It's usually always there, not on the surface, but underneath. The image is the same as always, dark hair, straight nose that lifts slightly at the tip, freckles across my nose and the dimple in my chin. I close my eyes and let go, like always I imagine water pouring over me again like it just did in the shower. I imagine it erasing the façade, exposing the truth beneath. When I open my eyes and look in the mirror, my eyes widen, because it's harder to see now. The brokenness, the sorrow, the grief, they're already growing fainter. In their place are small scars, battle scars that show how far I've come. I smile, I wear them proudly, they're proof that I can weather any storm, and that in the end, love prevails.

I will no longer be broken.

After only a few days with Cole, and a night spent making new commitments, agreements, promises, plans for our future, and talking about our hopes and dreams, for the first time in years, I'm confident that the pieces are going to be reassembled. The remaining cracks will mend, and that wholeness will be found once more. I know it will, because I have hope.

"Tatum?" Cole calls out from the bedroom.

I open the door, "I'm here," I reply.

"Are you okay?"

I look at myself in the mirror again and smile. "I'm great," I tell him.

"Then get your ass back to bed, woman!"

With a laugh, I run back to him to do just that.

EPILOGUE

Cole

Two Months Later

"Ten more reps and then you can go."

"You said that three sets ago," I complain to Jax, but he only smiles while the other guys gathered around watching like I'm a working exhibit, chuckle. With a sigh, obeying like a well-trained puppy. I lie back on the bench and count out each pump of the weight he's placed on the bar ten more times. When I'm finished I catch my breath, waiting for him to utter his next instructions before he dismisses me for the day.

Jax is taking his new role as my trainer very seriously. He's been working me hard for the last couple months, and while I wouldn't tell him this, I've loved every second of it. It's a whole different ballgame when training with someone that doesn't only point out the things you need to work on, but also tells you what you're doing right. Someone that doesn't scream insults at you the whole time you're training and gives you guidance and advice on how to become better. I've found my love for the sport again, and it feels great. I'm a new man, in more ways than one.

"Alright, you're done for the day, you can go now, but be back here first thing in the morning."

"Yes, sir," I tell him and salute with a big smile for good measure.

He shakes his head and I jet off to the locker room to take a quick shower before heading home to my girl. When I emerge, the guys are all standing around trying to be inconspicuous but are failing miserably. All of them. And at that thought, I smile. A few weeks ago Jax, Ryder and I sat Zane, Levi, Tyson, and Dylan down and told them the truth about Jerry and what had happened. I didn't spare any detail; I laid it all out for them to judge and ridicule to their heart's content. They had waited patiently until I was ready to share; no pushing or demanding the details, knowing the whole time that something was up given the amount of time I started spending here. But rather than lecturing or being angry, they were all supportive. They've given me shit at times, but each have taken time to privately encourage me, letting me know that they want to see me succeed and be happy. As if that wasn't enough, Jax made it clearly known to everyone again that Jerry is not allowed to take one step inside the gym and that if he tries, he's to be notified immediately. If he's not present then the task of kicking him out falls on one of the other guys. I have a feeling they would fight for the privilege.

Admittedly, it wasn't what I had expected. I had envisioned they would perhaps tell me how stupid I was; think I deserved the treatment I received given my inability to trust them. Or at a minimum, to give me shit for never asking for help. I'm not really sure but they never did any of that. Nope, I've received nothing but compassion and reassurance from all of them. I feel guilty that I expected anything less. As I consider how they've all rallied around me, it makes me grateful to have them for friends. It hasn't gone unnoticed or unappreciated that they've all been spending more time at the gym too, particularly when I'm here. They're all being protective, but of course they would deny it if mentioned, so I don't. Tatum says guys are weird, but I don't know what she means. Seems perfectly normal to me.

"What's going on?" I ask them all.

They all look to Jax, so I do too and see that he's holding papers in his hands. Old habits kick in automatically and my stomach turns over and I begin to worry, expecting the worse. The anxiety about what's about to happen must translate to my face because Jax is quick to reassure me, "It's nothing bad."

"Okay," I nod, swallow hard, and take a deep breath. I guess part of me is waiting for the other shoe to drop, things are going great – maybe too great. "Then what's going on?"

"I have some papers I need you to sign."

"For what?" I mentally slap myself knowing that I sound annoyed. Change does not come quickly or easily, I realize, as I hear Jax continue, unruffled by my response.

"Well, I've been thinking, you never got the chance to know my…our…grandfather - Jerry's father. I know you've heard me say that he was a good man. Nothing like Jerry." Jax has always called Jerry by name. He's never called him dad or father or even referred to him in that role. "Knowing him like I did, if he were still alive, he would have been thrilled by the news that he has another grandson. He'd be here every day, by my side, helping coach you, cheering you on every step of the way. And he'd attend every fight. He would have been the positive influence in your life that Jerry will *never* be, could never be. And so like I said, it got me thinking, and I know that had he known about you, he also would have left you this gym. We would be joint owners. Brothers in the business."

I begin shaking my head, thinking I have an idea of where this is going, but he ignores me and keeps talking. "And so, I had these papers drawn up because the right thing to do is to make you part owner now."

"Jax, no. That's not at all necessary. I don't want to share ownership of your business. It's not your fault; not your responsibility to take care of me just because…Jerry fathered me. This is not at all something you have to do."

There are some murmurs from the guys, but I don't hear them, my complete focus on Jax. "But that's just it, Cole. You are not something that is defined by a 'fault', or being a burden. You are not a mistake. I know I don't have to take care of you. None of that applies."

"But, Jax-"

He holds up his hands, "No, don't you get it? "Hell Cole, you are one of the only good things that son of a bitch has ever done in his life. We both are, if I do say so myself. You're my brother, and because of that, I want you to share the ownership of this gym with me. And truly, you deserve it every bit as much as I do."

"Look, you're the business guy, the coach, the head of our pack. You sure you don't want to do a DNA test or something…just to be sure? I mean, you don't have to do this. I really feel caught off guard here," mumbling and bumbling, unsure of what to say, I look down and move invisible objects with my feet.

"First, no I don't need a DNA test. Your mother confirmed it and ever since we found out, it's almost embarrassing we never noticed the similarities before. Secondly, I know I don't have to do this; I want to. It's a no-brainer. All the guys, they know about it too which is why they are here. Look around you," he says gesturing to the guys and I look at all of their smiling faces. "We are all excited and we want to celebrate. It's the right thing to do – and hell – I could use the help. I'd love it. And third, I know I've caught you off guard, if you need time to think about it, that's fine. Take these papers with you. Look them over when you have time to yourself, talk it over with Tatum, hell, take them to an attorney to look over. Do whatever you need to do, and then sign the fuckers so we can all go out to drink and celebrate. Got it?"

"Yeah, okay. I'll do that," I take the papers from him and hold them to my chest like they're breakable. It may be one of the best things that's ever happened to me.

"Okay, now, don't you have a pretty woman to get home to?" Jax asks.

"You know what? Hell yes, I do," I tell him with what I know is a huge ass smile on my face.

"You mean she hasn't come to her senses yet?" Levi asks.

"You wish, man," I reply.

"Yeah, actually, we both do," Zane says with a smile and at some level I kinda want to pound his face in.

"Keep your hands and eyes off of my woman or you'll lose them," I threaten.

Ryder laughs, "I like this version of Cole," he says to everyone. "He's badass again."

"It's true," Dylan chimes in. "I've got a boner from his threatening words."

The guys all laugh and I flip them all off and walk out the door. Hurrying to my car, I find myself anxious to get home to Tatum. She's been locked up in her little art room day and night all week long.

We wasted no time getting to Chicago and packing her up to get her permanently set up here. In the few days before we left to gather her things, everything fell into place; we found a new apartment, signed a lease, and started packing up my apartment. Ryder was pissed to see me move, but he understood our desire to start over - a new place, a fresh start. We found the perfect place, enough rooms that she has an art studio and I have a room for a few weights. We have more than enough money to live on between her art business and the money I've saved over the years. I saved every damn penny I could that didn't go to Jerry, and I've got quite the nice nest egg. Now, with the prospect of owning part of the gym, Tatum and I will be more than fine, and it feels like things are continuing to fall into place.

In between coordinating our move, we attended her gallery show in California, and it went really well. It was nice to see her family again, and the surprised looks on their faces when they saw me, was pretty entertaining. The rest of her tour she insisted on cancelling. She was no longer comfortable with the connection the tour had to

Blaine, and the fact it was obtained through his friend. I told her it didn't bother me one bit, but she insisted it bothered her, especially when we looked at our calendar and saw a couple stops I wouldn't be able to attend due to fights Jax has lined up. She stated she has no desire to attend without me. I'm not going to argue with that.

The last couple months have felt a little bit like a dream, and sometimes I'm afraid I'm going to wake up from it and find out it was all a tease instead – that would be a horrible nightmare. Those thoughts fade away more and more each day and being together has slowly become our new normal. And it's perfect and everything I hoped it would be.

My mom and I are doing better. She feels ashamed for not telling me the full story and has times when she feels vulnerable. But she seems emotionally more healthy than I have seen her in years, if ever. Tatum and I have her over for dinner a lot and I love watching the two of them in the kitchen cooking together, talking and laughing. We're all healing, more and more every day.

Finally arriving home, I let myself inside and smile as I call out, "Van Gogh, I'm home."

Tatum darts out of the back room, a smile on her face, and jumps into my arms. I hold her to me tightly, then place her back on her feet, my gaze taking in her frame hotly. She's wearing one of my white t-shirts and little else. She's taken to painting in them, and I find that I like it. A lot. Her dark hair is piled on top of her head, some of it falling around her face, and there are a few splatters of paint on her shirt and a smear here and there on her face. "God, you look gorgeous," I tell her.

She smiles and kisses me briefly. "Well hello to you too," she says and when she pulls away I mutter a groan of protest.

"Come here," I demand.

"I will, but first, I have a surprise for you."

"Well hell, this seems to be the day for surprises."

"What do you mean?"

"I'll tell you later," I reply and place the paperwork I'm referring to on the table. "What surprise?"

"Follow me."

She leads the way into her art studio and my hands find their way up her legs and over her ass teasing her on the way, making her giggle. I love the sound of her laugh. I wish I could bottle it up, then reopen it and play it like my own personal music box whenever I want.

Inside her studio she has a sheet over a painting on an easel. She turns to face me and bites her bottom lip, a sign that she's nervous. It makes my brow furrow wondering why she's feeling that way. She's never nervous to show me her work. "What's wrong?"

"Nothing, I just, have something for you."

"A painting? Like as a gift?" I ask already smiling. I love it when she paints for me.

"Close your eyes," she instructs and I obey.

I can hear the whishing sound of cloth sliding over canvas as she removes the cover. I hear her take a deep breath and then her whispered, "Open your eyes."

When I do, they find her first and I frown a little at the worried look on her face, my eyes moving quickly to discover what's got her in this state. Before me is an image of a woman in profile, from the neck down. She's cradling her pregnant belly. Behind her but turned a little more outward is a shirtless man with his face buried in the woman's neck. He's got one arm wrapped around her protectively. I know immediately that the man and woman in the painting is Tatum and me. I smile at this representation of a happy time in our life, and take a step closer, devouring every detail. I remember vividly awaiting the birth of Hope, how excited we were, and I love that she's brought this memory back to life. Regardless of the outcome, it was still a beautiful moment that I'll always cherish. I start to turn to her to tell her this, when something suddenly catches my eye.

She's painted my tattoos meticulously. The attention to detail is amazing, but the thing that makes me inhale sharply is that she's painted every tattoo as they are on my body right now. The tattoos that I've gotten since we were apart are depicted, and prevalent on my side is the tattoo of Hope's name.

Snapping my head to her, I stutter over my words, finally spitting out one, "Tatum?"

"Cole?"

"Is this? What is…are you…am I crazy? Are you…?"

"I'm pregnant."

"You're…how…" Elation makes me smile immediately.

"We haven't exactly been careful. I've been on birth control but you know, it's not one hundred percent effective."

I take her in my arms and cup her face in my hands, "We're having a baby?" The excitement is there, bright and hot, but my smile falls a little when white hot fear passes through my body. I'm ashamed to find it there, to feel it at all, but I can't help it. I try to not let her see it at first, but then consider how far we've come and drop the armor. She smiles softly and brushes her thumb across my face.

"I know. Me too. I took about eight home tests and then went to the doctor, feeling a mixture of elation and fear."

"Why didn't you tell me? I would have come with you."

"I wanted to be sure first, and I wanted to surprise you. So much. I immediately knew how I would do it and I wanted the chance."

"I understand, and I love my surprise. Tell me what the doctor said."

"She said that everything looks really good. Healthy, and strong. She said they will monitor me closely given what happened with Hope, but that there's no reason for alarm. We have no reason to be fearful, although I imagine it's normal, but I figure we will take it one day at a time. We have each other, and my god Cole, we created life together again."

I nod, my eyes burning, "One day at a time," I repeat.

"Yes."

My hands run down her arms, my fingers entwine with hers, "I'm warning you, I'm going to be annoyingly protective," I admit.

"How is this different from any other day?"

"That's true, but you know what I mean."

"I do, and I wouldn't expect anything less."

"Tatum," I whisper. "I'm thrilled, I am, but full confession here, I'm also a bit scared."

"I know, me too. But, life moves forward, and this has happened for a reason, it's supposed to be, and you and I, our house of love is strong. We'll get through this, no matter what, okay?"

I smile at her 'house of love' reference, remembering the advice she told me my mother gave her. It's become a motto of ours of sorts I guess. She even painted a picture that hangs in our entry way with the words – Our Home is Love. "Promise me."

"I promise," she whispers and I'm not sure where it comes from, but peace and contentment runs through my body and I relax, knowing we are right where we are supposed to be, and I'm given clarity that causes me to believe we'll be okay. No matter what happens. We're stronger now, smarter, more trusting and loyal. We know what it feels like to lose each other and to come out on the other side.

"I love you," I tell her. "I love you so much."

"I love you too," she says and kisses me.

Lifting her up, her legs wrap around my waist and I walk forward until I can sit her on the table in the room. Lifting the shirt over her body, I growl when I find small scraps of lace beneath it. "You're beautiful," I tell her.

She lifts my shirt over my head and helps me get out of my clothing quickly. "Now," she says, and in seconds I'm inside of her, moving against her, reveling in the feeling of how right this is. As I move in and out, my eyes move from hers down her body, and rest on her stomach. Seeing a palette of paint on the desk beside us, I reach over and dip my finger in the red paint and draw a heart on her stomach. I feel anticipation, excitement, and contentment at Tatum's announcement, but the love, the love I feel, it trumps all of these and runs through me in waves.

As Tatum's hand comes to settle over mine, and her whisper of "I love you," reaches my ears, I know immediately that what I've heard is true. Things we lose have a way of coming back to us in the end. We've come full circle, and I can't wait to find out what life has in store for us, and our new family.

ACKNOWLEDGEMENTS

This book was a labor of love for me, and I hope that you enjoyed it, and I thank you for picking it up and giving it a chance. Please consider leaving a review as it is a big help to me. Thank you.

There are many people that I need to thank for helping me along this journey. Georgia Cranston, as always, I love being co-dependent with you. Our coffee dates are everything. Lauren Miller, Angela Corbett, Stephanie Brown, Jennifer Domenico, Mayra Statham, and Glorya Hidalgo, you always offer encouragement and remind me that I can do this anytime I'm doubting myself. While writing this book, when my block was awful and I was ready to give up, each of you were there for me in your own way, and I can't tell you how much it means to me, and how lucky I am to call you my friends. To my mom, you always remind me that what I'm doing matters, that it's special and you tell me how proud you are of me. Your opinion and those words mean more to me than you could ever know. Thank you for taking the time to edit my words for me.

Thank you Robin Harper - You always hit it out of the ballpark with my covers, this is my favorite so far. But I say that after every one you design. Elaine York, you always make time for me no matter what, thank you for making me feel special, and making my books look beautiful.

To my husband and girls, thanks for your patience while I struggled to get through this story. I know there were many nights you were ignored, ate cereal for dinner, watched the house get dirty and saw your clothes sit unwashed for longer than normal, LOL! I love you, and I'm lucky to have you.

To my dad and Tami, thank you for showing me how beautiful love can be in the face of pain. While your circumstances are different, thoughts of you were prevalent throughout this story's journey. I love you both so much.

To all my readers, bloggers and my reader group, I couldn't do this without you. Thank you to each and every one of you.

ABOUT THE AUTHOR

Author Jennifer Miller was born and raised in Chicago, Illinois but now calls Arizona home. Her love of reading began when she was a small child, and only continued to grow as she entered adulthood. Ever since winning a writing contest at the young age of nine, when she wrote a book about a girl with a pet unicorn, she's dreamed of writing a book of her own. The important lesson she learned about dreams is that they don't just fall into your lap – you have to chase them yourself. Most importantly, she is a wife and mother, and is very lucky to have a family that loves and supports her in all things. She also has an unhealthy addiction to handbags and chocolate covered strawberries, neither of which she cares to work on. For more information about Jennifer Miller, please visit www. jennifermillerwrites.com.

Facebook – https://www.facebook.com/JenMillerWrites?ref=hl
Twitter – https://twitter.com/JenMillerWrites
Pinterest – http://www.pinterest.com/jenmillerwrites/
Sign up for my newsletter – http://goo.gl/JNRarR
Instagram - http://instagram.com/jenmillerwrites
Goodreads - https://www.goodreads.com/author/show/7019978.
Jennifer_Miller
Amazon Author page - http://amzn.to/1DzbfUH

BOOKS BY JENNIFER MILLER

Pretty Little Lies

Pretty Little Dreams

Pretty Little Vows - A Novella

Perfect Little Plan

Whispering Wishes

Charming

Fighting Envy

Fighting Wrath

Fighting Lust